Miracle on Deck 34 and other Yuletide Tales

Kaki Olsen

Kaki Olsen

Scott Ashby

Table of Contents

Publications by Kaki Olsen i

Books by Scott Ashby ii

Introduction iii

Silent Night, Holey Night 1

Miracle on Deck 34 9

Hark, Harold the Angel Sings 17

Once On Royal David's Planet 25

Santa Claus is Coming to Titan 31

A Visit From NK-LAS 39

The Nearly Lost Gift of The Magi 43

I'll Be On-Station for Christmas 51

O Tannin Bomb 59

Away In A Mess Hall 67

Away in a Spaceship 75

I Heard the Engines on Christmas Day 83

One More Cryosleep 'Til Christmas 91

We Three Little Green Kings 99

Rudolph, the Red-Bulbed Recon Drone 103

Rock-ing Around the Christmas Tree.........................111

I Wonder As I Wander Out Among the Stars 119

O Little Moon of Death, Mayhem 125

Joy to the Other Otherworld.......................................131

Red Shirts Roasting on an Open Fire.........................135

Hover-sleigh Ride 143

It's the Most Wonderful Time for the Fear.................151

I Saw Three Spirits Come Phasing In 157

Sleep in Kryosleep Peace...167

About the Authors 175

Connect with us online...176

Publications by Kaki Olsen

Swan and Shadow: A Swan Lake Story
"Just One Chance" (Found in *Iron Doves: A Charity Anthology)*
"Ethical Will" (Found in *Unspun: A Collection of Tattered Fairy Tales)*
"Cultivation" (Found in *Something Found)*
"Among the Stars" (Found in *Something Lost)*
"Lost in Interpretation" (Found in *Get Your Book Published: 10 Authors, 10 True Stories, 10 Ways to Get Your Book Published)*
"Branch 9 3/4" *(*Found in *Mormon Lit Blitz Anthology: Volume 1: The First Five Years 2012-2016)*

Books by Scott Ashby

The Kwennjurat Chronicles
Tanella's Flight
The Siege of Kwennjurat

The Cavaliers
Assignment to Earth
Encounter at Kiral
Destruction at Decima
Perilous Patrol
Terror on Terradia
Court-Martial on the Charys
The Timorans

Other Titles
Mind Touch
Crown of Tears
Fabric of the World

Anthologies
Bits and Bites
Miracle on Deck 34 and Other Yuletide Tales

Introduction

I have long been a fan of Christmas tales, ranging from O. Henry's "The Gift of the Magi" or Chris Van Allsburg's *The Polar Express*. I cry at *It's a Wonderful Life* every year and read A Christmas Carol. While I find a place to sing or play Handel's *Messiah* whenever possible, I appreciate my Aunt Nedra, who sends me a new book for Advent every year. The themes are timeless and the resolutions profoundly moving to me.

Several months ago, I had just watched *The Muppet Christmas Carol* when I recalled a book I had read in high school. I cannot now name the author or the title after the passage of some years, but it answered some uncommon questions about the Bible and one was "Do Christians believe in aliens?" The answer quoted the message that, "other sheep I have, which are not of this fold"(John 10:16). It caused me to consider ways in which holiday fiction could transcend not only time, but location.

I whimsically wished on social media that I could find stories of the holidays in speculative fiction with titles like "Miracle on Deck 34" or "One More Cryosleep 'Til Christmas."

I didn't realize at first that Scott's prompting for more titles meant that he was planning something more than a brainstorm with these musings. I was delighted when I found a proposed anthology with those titles sent to my inbox.

These stories are varied in tone and theme, but I feel as though they recall the words of the Ghost of Christmas Present, written by Paul Williams for the Muppets: "It's true, whenever you find love, it feels like Christmas." I hope you enjoy this advent calendar of Yuletide tales.

– Kaki Olsen

When Kaki posted her wish on Facebook for stories with titles like "Miracle on Deck 34", my daughter and I started coming up with titles that were take-offs on Christmas Carols. In that moment, I had no plans other than the fun of coming up with titles. Kaki added more titles, and we added more. By the end of the evening, there was a whole thread of titles, and my fingers started itching to write them…but this was Kaki's project, and I didn't feel I could just go ahead without her approval and cooperation.

I wrote Kaki and proposed the anthology as a story-reading advent calendar, and she thought it was a great idea. Then I pitched it to my publishers at The Electric Scroll, and they got behind it as well. And that's how an idle Facebook post became a novel-length anthology, with a short story every day from December first until Christmas Eve. I hope you enjoy reading them as much as we enjoyed writing them.

– Scott Ashby

Miracle on Deck 34 and other Yuletide Tales

Silent Night, Holey Night

Scott Ashby

The *Galileo* was still drifting as it exited the gate from Q-75, the artificial wormhole. Using engines during a wormhole transit, natural or artificial, invariably messed up the transit and you never knew where you might come out.

The trick was to build up speed in the right direction so that when the hole opened, you had to cut power or else risk drifting neatly into the opening.

As the *Galileo's* helmsman, I was alone on the deck. I waited until I saw the wormhole exit finish closing before I even reached for the controls that would fire the engines back up. I'd seen a ship start up too soon, once, and get flipped into who-knew-where, because the wormhole was still open. That ship was still missing.

We had to cross a corner of the quadrant to the entrance of Q-4, one of the two naturally occurring wormholes in the area.

Before my hands got to the controls, there was a thump, and the ship shuddered slightly. I could hear – no, feel – no, that wasn't right either, but I knew there was something going wrong.

My eyes scanned the control panels, but every light was the proper color, and nothing was flashing, beeping, or otherwise complaining. Still, there was something wrong, I could feel it.

I ran my left hand over the cockpit wall. It was…tingling was the best word I could come up with.

Captain Charbro came onto the bridge and took his seat. Well, it was called the bridge, but it was really just a cramped little space. One seat for driving, one for scanning and navigating, and a third, where the captain could sit to boss us around. He didn't have to ask us for information, because he could see our panels over our shoulders. Ancient airline pilots had more room.

"What's happening, Skip? Did we hit something?"

So, the thump hadn't been in my imagination.

"Apparently not. No signs of damage. We were still in drift when it happened. Whatever *it* was."

Charbro leaned over my shoulder and looked at all the information the panel was displaying. "Everything looks in order."

"Yeah, it does. But it doesn't feel right. Put your hand on the wall."

The captain's hand didn't linger. "Yeah, I see what you mean."

He moved to the seat in front of the other set of controls and started flicking switches. As captain, his job was to give the orders, but he'd worked every job on the ship; not to the point of mastery, but to competency, to where he could fill in in any vital job and do it well enough to keep people breathing. That was one of the reasons I'd turned down several promotions to stay on with Charbro.

He sat in silence, gathering information about both the ship and the immediate vicinity, and then he groaned.

"Where in tarnation did that thing come from?"

"What thing?" I asked.

"The thud and shiver was us colliding with the gravity well of a black hole."

I shuddered. We were dead. "Can we still go around? Give me a course."

Captain Charbro shook his head. "Try 3-1-6, mark 15, it's our best shot. And I'll get a message off. Q-75 shouldn't be used again. The exit's just too near this thing. Where *did* it come from? And on Christmas Eve, too."

I pointed the *Galileo* in the direction the captain had given me, ramping the engines up as fast as I could without letting the passengers experience the surge of acceleration that would worry them.

Keeping the voyage smooth was more important. It would only take a couple of seconds more to avoid scaring the passengers, and those seconds wouldn't make a difference in our dubious ability to escape the black hole's clutches.

When the engines first engaged, I thought we might have a chance. There was a small thud and a shiver, nearly identical to the one I'd felt just after we'd come through the wormhole.

I piled on more and more power until the ship's engines were well beyond their advertised operational capacity. I wasn't sure what safety margin had been designed into the engines, but it hardly mattered. We would either burn out the engines and escape, then drift until rescue came, or we'd fall past the event horizon and die in agony as we were slowly stretched and compressed into a long strand of atoms. I was sure spaghettification was a process I wouldn't enjoy, even if I lived to experience it…which, of course, I wouldn't. The ship, in shrinking and being pulled, would break apart much sooner than my somewhat elastic body, and I'd die, swiftly, along with the three thousand passengers and thousand crew members on the ship, from the oxygen rushing through the hull breach.

Some of the crew were too new to feel there was something wrong with the *Galileo*, but the older hands would know. They'd feel the tension in the air, the trembling of a ship that didn't want to die. Some of the passengers would have been on enough cruises to be able to feel that there was something else happening, but the vast majority would go to their deaths not knowing what was going on, and would enjoy their last few minutes, hours, days, as the *Galileo* was dragged, kicking and screaming, into the final abyss at an ever-increasing speed.

Some scientists hypothesized that falling over the event horizon was like exceeding the speed of light, although no one had ever managed to live to make the comparison.

Others claimed that a black hole was merely a super-powerful wormhole, taking you someplace else, although no one knew where.

The demonstrable fact was that, despite all the theory and speculation, no one knew. Black holes were akin to death – no one had ever come back to tell us what, if anything, was on the other side.

I wasn't really interested in finding out. I'd settle for a miraculous intervention; angels, demons, saints, gods…I didn't much care who staged the intervention, so long as it ended with me – and my passengers – remaining on this side of the hole.

A shadow passed over the cockpit window, blotting out some of the stars. The silhouette wasn't the sleek shape of another starship, but I couldn't really figure out what it was.

It appeared to be some sort of open-topped box, holding…no, my eyes must be going already, in the grip of the black hole.

"Do you see it, too?" Captain Charbro asked.

"I see…well, I'm not really sure what it is, but it's tickling the memories in the back of my childhood."

"It's some sort of conveyance," Charbro said, "though not one that's familiar to me."

"It looks like it's open to space," I added.

"Did you see the guy driving it?"

"Well, somewhat. He looked lively and quick."

A slight humming sound alerted us that we were no longer alone. We turned toward the back of the bridge, and there he stood, the man from the unusual conveyance, having apparently teleported in without authorization, a dangerous enough proposition with both ships stationary relative to each other, which we weren't. So…who was driving his ship? It had looked like he was alone.

He was dressed in white-trimmed red fur from head to toe, and the suit had picked up a ton of black, carbonish particles someplace.

He seemed to be in a state of perpetual happiness, down to the twinkling eyes and dimples. His nose and cheeks were red from cold, possibly from being unprotected in an open vehicle in space.

Unprotected in space? We must be deeper into that black

hole than the instruments showed.

He sported a white beard and mustache so thick that if it weren't for the pipe, you'd never be able to find his mouth.

And there was another strange thing, although smoke from the pipe twined up and circled around his head, it wasn't setting off any of the combustion alarms.

Whoever the guy was, he was a fat little thing; I'd never seen anyone with enough fat to actually jiggle, but he was managing it.

"S-Santa?" Captain Charbro asked, his voice barely above whisper. Of course, that brought my memories to the fore, and I realized the guy did look exactly like Santa should, and as I looked out the window, his ship was revealed to be a sleigh, pulled by horned horses. No, the poem called them reindeer, didn't it? It was absolutely insane, but then, people who are being sucked into black holes are thought to go mad before they are pulled apart by the forces within. As though scientists could know what people are thinking when they're standing in the same room with them, much less hypothetical people being sucked into a black hole.

The little old man (if he was a man, because the legends were so old that the guy, if he ever existed, must be long dead by now) placed one white-gloved finger over his lips, in a soundless request for silence.

He stepped to my board and made a course and power change, and then, and I swear this is how it happened, he simply vanished. There one moment, gone the next.

I sat back down at the control panel, and Captain Charbro came over and glanced at the controls.

The course Santa had set led straight into the center of the black hole, at a power setting that should have been far beyond the capabilities of the *Galileo*.

Icy sweat broke out all over my body, and I reached to change the settings. This course was a one-way trip to the cemetery.

Before I could reach the controls, Captain Charbro's fingers wrapped firmly around my wrist.

"No. If we're going to die, let's make it quick. And otherwise, we'll assume that Santa knows what he's doing. Leave the controls alone."

I nodded. I didn't agree with the order, but Captain Charbro had never steered me wrong, and a career-long habit of obeying him held, as I faced the awful eye of the hole, and, incredibly, followed the red sleigh into oblivion.

I came to myself, still belted in my seat. The *Galileo* was drifting in space, all engines off.

A bright star shone through the window, nearly blinding me. I put on a visor and continued scanning my board.

Nothing seemed amiss. The black hole was gone. We were where we should have been had we passed through Q-4. I glanced at the scanner, but couldn't see the wormhole behind me, so it must have closed while I was…unconscious. Yes, I'd write in my report that I had been rendered unconscious. It would read better than that I'd fallen asleep at my post.

Captain Charbro got up from where he had fallen to the floor.

He looked around, then laid eyes on the chronometer.

"Christmas morning," he grunted. Then he looked sharply at me.

"Did you see…him…too?"

I smiled.

"What, did I see Santa Claus come flying up out of the middle of outer space and rescue us all from a black hole that shouldn't have been where it was?"

Captain Charbro went pasty white as I'd spoken.

"I didn't see it if you didn't, sir."

He flashed a shy shadow of a grin at me as he sat in his seat.

"Good thing neither of us saw it, then, isn't it?"

There would be no report, then, of course, since neither of us saw anything, but I knew I'd spend the rest of my life wondering if it had truly happened, or if I'd had a rather interesting, shared dream after having too much Christmas dinner.

Miracle on Deck 34

Kaki Olsen

Julia was absolutely sure she lived in the best place in the solar system. Mrs. Ellis had said as much in history class, but Julia stole an infochip from the visitor's center to learn about some of the things a teacher wouldn't think to mention. It was the chip that informed her that her birthplace was Waypoint Station: Last Stop On the Way Home.

Thanks to that chip, she could find every public bathroom and give directions to the Council offices. She discovered that 247 kids had been born on-station, even though only fourteen were here now. Everyone who came here knew she was one of the 247 and that made her immediately interesting.

Arrivals was practically a station holiday and the last one had been three months ago. School let out early so the teachers could help with new student enrollment.

Julia wasn't needed at home. Mom was in her office at Family Services until four and Dad was almost always tied up in Engineering until six. Jonah was in daycare and Joseph would be on the basketball court after school, so she was free to do what Mom always called goggling.

Mom couldn't blame her for wanting to people-watch. When you had one other kid your age and saw the same people every day, any chance for someone new was an awesome thing.

Besides, she didn't *goggle*. She stood just past Customs and looked for kids who could use a tour guide.

"Coming through or staying?" she asked a boy Jonah's age.

"Coming through," he answered distractedly before running to catch up with his parents at the map.

It took her two more tries before someone stopped to talk to her. The girl had the darkest hair Julia had ever seen and was, for some reason, alone. Julia's possible new acquaintance spent a whole minute staring at the Arrivals Hall and didn't seem to hear the question at first.

"Staying?" the girl echoed. "You can *stay* here?"

"Of course," Julia said, trying not to laugh at the wide-eyed expression. "It's not just bots who live here."

She couldn't remember the number of bots per human, but the robots were all helping at the warehouses or the engineering decks.

"I'm Julia," she added. "I'm nine and I live on Deck 22."

"Silva," the other girl responded. "I'm nine and our ship doesn't even *have* a Deck 22."

"Boy, are you in luck!" Julia announced with a grin.

Two minutes later, she'd found out that Silva had already eaten lunch, didn't need a bathroom, was curious about the market, and definitely wanted to see the garden on Deck 50.

"Where do you want to go first?" Julia asked.

Silva suddenly looked a little embarrassed; maybe she

thought she'd sound stupid. "Where's Santa?"

Julia's first thought was to say, "Earth's North Pole, dummy," but she'd decided as Genius Guide that there were no stupid questions. Instead of breaking her personal rule, she said, "Is that someone who lives here?"

"They said he's here," her new friend said earnestly. "Nicholas..."

"Oh!" She'd never thought of the quartermaster as Santa, but she supposed it was as good a nickname as any. "He works on Deck 34."

Nicholas lived by school on Deck 19 and his directory listing said he was the supervisor over all the warehouse levels. His office was on Deck 34, two doors to the right of the elevators.

"Come on," she said. "I'll introduce you."

She went to Port Elevator 3– it was the one with the best view of the world below—-but they didn't have much time to stare out the glass window for long before the doors opened onto Deck 34. Silva didn't look out the window at the distance between them and the continents below. She bounced nervously from one foot to the other and watched the numbers flash on the panel. Julia found herself almost humming with shared excitement.

31...

32...

33...

The doors slid open on Deck 34, which was just like every other deck. A list of offices and a map of compartments was on one wall and long, boring hallways. She had been here once for a field trip and last year for a new bed, but it hadn't changed at all. She let Silva leave first, then turned smartly to the right and walked past the emergency aid closet to Nicholas' door.

"Julia Vanderkamp." The old man's voice was booming and laughing and perfect for his ear-to-ear smile. "I don't see Jonah or Joseph with you, so this must be Jane?" he teased.

Julia glanced back at Silva, who was smiling for the first time since they'd met. "Silva Noelle," she answered. "Are you..."

"Jolly Old Nicholas?" he asked. "That's one of my names. And I know your name."

"You couldn't," Julia protested. "She just *got* here."

"True, true." He winked at them each in turn. "I know you're Silva Noelle from the *Excelsior*, like Zoe Patterson and Josue Orellano and Mei Nguyen and thirty-three other children. As it is, I'm very pleased to meet you."

"Anything you need, Nicholas can find," Julia explained while the other two shook hands. "Beds, chairs, stoves, fabrics for the tailors, salt for the cooks. If he doesn't have it, he can find it for you. Just like magic."

"Is that true?" Silva asked, wide-eyed.

"Julia Vanderkamp knows me better than I know myself." Nicholas paused to ruffle the hair of the visitor he'd known the longest. "What is it you're looking for, Silva?"

The embarrassed look came back to Silva's face and she looked quickly at Julia before staring very intently at her shoes. Julia picked up the hint and quickly backed away.

"I'll be by the elevator when you're ready to go."

Everyone knew that a visit to any Santa was between you and him. No exceptions.

"Emergency meeting," Mom called on her way in the door. She pulled leftovers from the fridge and handed them to Joseph. "Dad will be home soon, so just keep an eye on each other…"

"…And make sure everyone eats their vegetables," Julia's older brother finished. "I'll make sure we all behave ourselves."

"I know you will."

She stopped in her home office long enough to swap some of her files for others and pick up a battery pack for her tablet. By the time she was back at the door, Julia had found her a protein bar to eat on the way back to her office. Mom thanked her with a kiss to the forehead, then called goodbye to the other two. Jonah was too engrossed in a new game to respond.

Julia glanced at her brother as soon as the door closed. "Do you know what the emergency is?"

"No clue," Joseph answered. "Maybe something with one of the arrivals."

Dad gave the same answer half an hour later, then changed the subject to her math test the next day. She ran through the drills with him until she felt like answering Jonah's question about dessert with a fraction.

When the drills were over, she had to do her reading for the next day. Her thoughts went back to Mom's emergency meeting and the only answer anyone seemed to be giving her about it. There hadn't been any signs of a problem when she and Silva explored the station, and no one had stopped Silva from going back to her ship for the night.

Silva wasn't one of the new students introduced the next morning. There was another girl Julia's age – the Zoe Patterson who Nicholas had mentioned – but there wasn't time for a lot of questions until lunch. Julia shared her cookie from home and tried to be as subtle as possible.

Towards the end of lunch, when Julia had heard about Zoe's older sister Annie and how Mrs. Patterson was the new music teacher and Mr. Patterson was a lawyer, she slipped in a question that had nothing to do with her new classmate.

"I don't know," Zoe said, looking surprised. "She wasn't on the list of people staying, but she said she wanted to."

"Don't her parents decide?"

Zoe's only answer was a shrug. Mrs. Ellis called them back to the classroom a moment later, so all mysteries would have to wait until after last bell.

Mom had no emergency meetings that night, but she explained that they were trying to find a home for a child who had not been an orphan when her family set out for their new home. She never spoke the child's name, but her eyes darted to Julia more than once and Julia immediately promised herself that she'd find Silva the next day to ask some more questions.

After last bell, Mrs. Ellis held the class back for a minute. "Zoe has been instructed to go to Nicholas' office," she announced. "Julia, will you show her the way?"

Nicholas might have more information on Silva than Julia's new classmate, so she agreed immediately.

"Santa presents," Zoe explained once they were out of the classroom.

It wasn't a name normally mentioned around her and this was the second time in as many days that someone had brought him up. "What do you mean?"

"We were all told to think of something we really wanted for when we arrived and request them before we got here,"

Zoe elaborated. "The little kids called them Santa presents."

"What did you ask for?"

Zoe's smile was nervous. "We'll see if he has it."

Nicholas welcomed them and sent Julia off with one of the Labor Functionary bots to find container 22114.

"She called this her Santa present," Julia commented once the LF and her new friend had disappeared around a corner.

"Many children do," he said, stroking his white beard.

"And Silva called you Santa."

He glanced at her with one eyebrow raised to silently ask her to get to the point.

"But you're not Santa."

"I never said that."

"But Silva and Zoe think you're him." He simply hummed in response, and she sighed impatiently. "But he's not real."

"He's a kind man who can give them any gift that they can think of," Mr. Nicholas said. "I think I'm pretty close."

"What did Silva ask for?"

"That's between me and her," he replied solemnly, "but it's certainly a challenging request."

Zoe returned with a grin almost as wide as Nicholas' and an aquarium. "I'm to go to Deck 17," she announced.

"And I think Stall 44," Nicholas added. "They should have everything you need."

"*Thank* you," Zoe effused before turning and hugging Jolly Old Nicholas' LF.

"Do you want me to – "

"I can find it," Zoe called over her shoulder as she almost ran to the elevator.

"First time I've ever been asked for a pet goldfish,"

Nicholas confided in Julia. "She read about them in a book. Your friend Silva asked me another first."

"And you won't say what…"

"It's her secret to tell."

She didn't ask for the secret again, but she left a request of her own before leaving.

Mom and Dad were both home when the Vanderkamp kids returned from school the next day.

"There's a new arrival who has no wish to go, but nowhere to stay," Dad said once they were all seated. "We have discussed it with the Council and wanted to ask your thoughts before offering her a place in our family."

"Silva," Julia guessed immediately.

Mom, whose emergency meetings must have been about this very need, nodded solemnly. "Her parents both died on their way here and someone here made her feel at home, so she changed her mind about continuing the journey."

It took very little convincing for the two sides of a new family to come to an agreement and Silva arrived the next morning.

"You asked Santa for a home," Julia guessed. At the look of astonishment on Silva's face, she grinned. "Don't worry. He didn't tell me."

Years ago she had asked Santa for a sister, but only Jolly Old Nicholas, of Deck 34 had been real enough to simultaneously grant two wishes.

Hark, Harold the Angel Sings

Scott Ashby

'm sorry, Harold, it isn't that you're not good, it's just that you're too…"

Small, Harold finished the sentence in his mind along with the choir director. He didn't know what his size had to do with his ability to sing, except that it made the choir look bad; unbalanced, one choir director had said. They all wanted their choirs to be filled with what they felt were 'mighty angels'; big, competent angels. Angels who could deliver a message and then enforce the dictates of Heaven should the mortals seem disinclined to obey.

Harold sighed. It wasn't like he had any ambition to be one of the official Herald Angels, those who went out and about on Heaven's business, making startling announcements to mortals. Most of them came back and laughed, anyway. "You should have seen his face! Nineveh, I ask you!"

Not that Gabriel had been disrespectful when he'd made his announcement to Mary…not even when he'd had to go back and explain it to Joseph, to keep him from divorcing her; no, Gabriel hadn't so much as snickered.

Hark, Harold the Angel Sings

No, Harold didn't want to be important. He didn't want a solo, even, he just wanted to sing.

Most of the angel choirs, for all their practicing, only sang at church every week, anyway.

They just wanted to look good because there were rumors that the best of the choirs were going to be asked to sing at the big event that was coming up soon, to celebrate the mortal birth of the Savior.

Harold was used to friends going off to be born, live, and go on, and they all had plans to meet each other after they'd all had time to live and to die. Still, he missed some of his favorite friends. He'd been pretty close with Jesus.

Well, he supposed everyone felt that way. Jesus always had time for everyone, time to listen to their troubles, and time to just be together. He'd made time to make everyone feel important.

Harold knew it would be a long while before it was his turn to be born – he was being saved for the last days, though he hadn't learned the details of his mission yet. Nobody properly knew, until just before they left, to keep them from feeling anxious about whether or not they felt like they could do the job. Harold shrugged. He'd do the job because he'd be given the talents and had been told he'd need to do it. Father never made anything easy, but he always made it possible.

No, Harold didn't want to be important, he just wanted to sing. He loved music so much; it was almost the most important thing in his life, other than his love for Father's plan, and his now-on-hold friendship with Jesus.

Harold graciously thanked the choir director for his time, and turned away, walking off down the street. The problem was, that angel was the last choir director in heaven. Harold had tried them all, and none of them wanted him. And every one who'd rejected him had admitted he sang well enough, but was disqualified because of his size. Too small, too short, too wizened, too...everything! They were fixated on their choir being perfect in every way, and he just didn't fit the mold of the perfect angel.

Harold sighed again as he walked down the street. He wished Jesus was here; he'd help him think of a solution. He was so busy being dejected that he didn't look where he was going and blundered right into Joe. Though Jesus had been first-born to their heavenly parents, Joe was probably one of the most important people here--he'd been picked to help with a very hush-hush job. Nobody knew what it was, but they all knew it was important. Harold was flustered to have caused any trouble to such an important angel.

"Whoa, there, Harold. What's the problem? You're usually not so clumsy."

Harold felt his cheeks burning with his shame. "Sorry, Joe, it's just that I've...I've..." It was no good, the words wouldn't come out.

Joe led him off to the side of the street, to a conveniently placed bench, sat, and indicated that Harold should also sit.

Yup that was Joe. Busy as he was, he, like Jesus, always made time for others. Harold resolved to be more like them both, so full of kindness.

"It's just that I was rejected from the last choir, and, well, I like singing, and making music. It's stupid to feel so bad, I know."

"No, it's rather stupid to have rejected you. You have a wonderful voice. Why are they rejecting you?"

"They don't like the way I look. They want symmetry in

19

their choirs, they want everyone to match. They're looking for 'mighty' angels, and, while there are lots of adjectives to describe me, mighty I'm not."

Joe wrinkled his nose. "I'm not very mighty either, but I'm good enough to get the job done. Why don't you just start your own choir?"

"Is that allowed?"

Joe laughed. "I don't see why not."

Harold spent the next little while finding people who'd been rejected from other choirs for their looks, and trying to find matching choir robes, of which there didn't seem to be any.

Rehearsals were splendid, if you simply listened to the choir and didn't look at them. Everyone just wore their best and sang what was in their heart.

Harold's choir practiced twice a week, the same as the other, more beautiful-looking choirs did. The others sang every week in church, but no congregation seemed to want Harold's choir to sing to them. Like most of the choirs, they had more than one musical offering they were practicing at the same time, in various stages of readiness, so that they were ready to perform something at any moment, but they also had other items at or near performance-ready status.

Some of Harold's choir members had choir robes in various shades and colors, leftovers from previous choirs they'd sung in. Many of Harold's volunteers were somewhat retired, their voices past their prime, but Harold didn't care. They made beautiful music together, and they had a lot of fun doing it, and that was all he cared about. Even Quasi, that poor fellow with back trouble, managed to sing. He had to sit while he sang, in order to get his lungs lined up right, but he had great enthusiasm, and the rough edges of his voice still blended with the other vocalists.

Three members of Harold's choir set themselves the task of scrounging choir robes for those individuals who didn't have any. Eventually, everyone had their own robe – although it was a solid fact that no two robes were the same design or color. They decided to call themselves Harold's Volunteers, and they were proud of Harold's number one rule: that no one who wanted to sing in his choir would be turned away.

Everyone in every choir was carefully watching the woman who carried their Savior, trying to guess at the day she would be delivered, while at the same time, they all pretended they weren't watching. Meanwhile, every choir practiced the music to be sung that night, while no one even questioned how their choir-masters had gotten hold of it.

Finally the day came, and the announcement went out that all the choirs of Heaven would be singing that evening.

All?

All!

That evening, the choirs assembled. Matching, glorious, gleaming white robes were issued to every choir as they assembled. Everyone knew their notes and the words, so just the timing was important.

Father himself arranged where everyone should stand, which was proper because he would be acting as choirmaster himself, this evening of all evenings.

The angel with the speaking part nervously stood by – he'd be going on first and had only one shot at getting everything right.

The woman labored, and eventually produced the Son they had all been waiting for since the beginning of the world.

Hark, Harold the Angel Sings

The shepherds were near the small town, taking care of their flocks – where else would they be?

The curtains between Heaven and Earth were swept aside, and lo, the angel of the Lord came upon the shepherds, and the glory of the Lord lit up the fields, and the shepherds were sore afraid – as who wouldn't be afraid if the night were suddenly day, and a guy was standing in the air; things they'd never seen before, and certainly hadn't thought possible.

And the Herald Angel said, "Fear not: for, behold, I bring you good tidings of great joy, which shall be to all people.

"For unto you is born this day in the city of David a Saviour, which is Christ the Lord."

Harold took a deep breath. It was almost time for them to go on, and Father had placed him and his Volunteers right in the center of the front, because of their loving attitude toward each other and toward the music.

"And this shall be a sign unto you;" the Herald Angel continued, "Ye shall find the babe wrapped in swaddling clothes, lying in a manger."

The secondary curtain was drawn aside, and suddenly, the shepherds could see and hear the choir, singing together, singing a song that praised God, and concluding the song with "Glory to God in the highest, and on earth peace, goodwill toward men." There were quite a few repetitions of the 'glory' and 'peace' phrases, in different keys and harmonies, and Harold thought it sounded wonderful.

The song finally ended, the curtains were re-drawn between the angel choir and the shepherds, and Harold sighed with the same great joy as the shepherds on earth were feeling. It hadn't mattered that he wasn't a 'mighty angel', or one of the 'herald angels'. It hadn't mattered that he was short.

Joe was right, he'd created his own choir, and they'd been honored because of their love of music and their love and acceptance of all those around them. He'd acted like he'd seen Jesus and Joe act, and it had paid off in the end.

Hark! Harold, the angel, had sung!

Once on Royal David's Planet

Kaki Olsen

n identical message went out to all of the clergy on board two days before Advent: *We thought it would be appropriate for you to share a festive message with the children.*

Attached was a calendar and before Ian Markham could check his schedule, dates began filling up. The first night of Hanukkah was the first to be claimed with Rabbi Edelman's usual enthusiasm. The soft-spoken German who kept up the 19th century tradition of erasing one chalk mark from his door for each day of Advent scheduled his visit for the Feast of Saint Nicholas. Another signed up for the second Sunday of Advent, but asked that the calendar be extended to the New Year so that Kwanzaa could be represented. He was given a second slot on December 26 to teach about the seven principles of African heritage.

Bishop Markham daringly entered his name for Christmas Eve and informed his wife that he'd be reading from the Gospels in the interdenominational Sunday School.

"They'll like that," Sarah commented. "One last reminder

of the spirit of the season before all the presents."

"What's not to like?" he retorted jovially. "Matthew has the three wise men and angelic warnings. Luke has heavenly hosts and a baby, lying in a manger. I'll bring in a bit of Thomas Hardy with the oxen kneeling and send them off to bed with 'Picture a Christmas' or 'Silent Night.'"

"And you'll be interrupted by someone talking about their annoying baby brother and another wanting to tell you what they asked Santa for," she predicted.

"Probably." Kids had a more interactive relationship with lessons, and he welcomed that. "No one will blame them for being a bit excited."

He was confident that the message would reach at least some of them. After all, the Christmas stories were classics that were beautiful expressions of faith in addition to being captivating tales.

Or so they had once been when things were not lost in interpretation.

Bishop Markham had not anticipated problems. Like the other clergy on board, he was friendly with children being raised in many religious traditions and accepted invitations to worship with other congregations on a regular basis. Each of his colleagues had an approach to ministering to the younger believers on this ship, but Markham was known for his willingness to answer any question as respectfully as possible. The children would respond to honesty and feel comfortable with raising other concerns as they grew up and he could think of no better way to minister.

The other teachers always took this approach in stride, even if it sometimes resulted in odd tangents or needing to abandon the original lesson plan. They knew he meant well and usually gave him the benefit of the doubt.

He didn't pay attention to the attendance numbers when he attended the others' presentations, but he knew that forty-seven kids came on December 24. By invitation, they were already in their pajamas and while it took some time for the teachers to calm them all down, two carols got them in the right mood before he was given their mostly-rapt attention.

He managed to make it through the decree that all the world should be taxed and the idea that Joseph and Mary were not assigned a housing unit before arriving in the mysterious colony of Bethlehem, but before they could get to the angel of the Lord coming to the shepherds, a hand went up in the first row.

"Flocks of what?"

Bishop Markham blinked at his copy of the Bible for a minute before identifying a beast unknown to this little flock: "Sheep."

"What kind of birds are those?"

He saw a few smiles being covered by hands in the teachers' row, but not one of the children mocked the question. Once they reached their new homes, scientists would make it possible for larger animals to become a commonplace sight. For now, he had to explain that the small birds brought along on this journey were not the only things that came in flocks and leave more complex zoology for another time. The inquirer took the explanation calmly, though he anticipated there would be a few students asking their parents if flocks of sheep were real or if they were a myth like unicorns.

Rather than inspiring awe, the description of the multitude of the heavenly host led to a worried cry of, "Which world did the angels come from?" and two follow-up questions. ("If it's peace on earth, do the angels not like any-one on other planets?" and "Does every planet have its own type of angel?")

More important than explaining sheep was assuring the children that God loved them just as much as people who shared a native planet with the Lamb of God. These were children traveling between the stars, who reckoned direction by fore and aft, port and starboard, and knew their planet of origin and destination. Some of them didn't even have a planet of origin, having been granted citizenship by the country that sponsored their parents' travel to a new world. They had the right to know that they were still made in the image of God and that the Christ child had been born for them on a planet they would probably never visit.

Markham was grateful to get through the visit of the wise men from the east without having to pull up a star chart or talk about why Herod had to consult the scribes instead of going into the citizen registration files. The footnotes for next year's reading were becoming longer than the text itself.

"I hear it went well," Sarah commented on his return.

"I think we got there in the end," Ian agreed. "I'd be curious to hear what each of them remembers tomorrow."

"That sheep are not like chickens," she predicted.

He wasn't sure how the word had spread to her ears in the ten minutes since he'd left the Sunday School classroom, but he flashed a self-deprecating smile at her and took the teasing in stride.

He went to sleep on Christmas Eve with a head full of cross-references and careful reassurances.

Had the chronicle of Christ's birth been assigned to a more practical man than an evangelist, the story of what came upon a midnight clear would have been couched in language that covered all explanations.

"And so it was, that while Mary and Joseph were participating in an in-person census decreed for all residents in the zoned municipal district historically associated with the biologically-descended and legally-associated family of David (registration number needs citation), the days were accomplished that she should be delivered and she was not registered with the corresponding medical center in the ZMD of Bethlehem. And she brought forth her firstborn son and wrapped him in swaddling clothes not obtained through the communal textile stores, and laid him in a manger because the public hostels were not adequately prepared for an influx of citizens from another ZMD and she had not applied for an emergency housing allowance under medical exception laws before traveling from her family's ZMD."

He couldn't stomach the Gospel of Luke sounding like a citation for trespassing, but it was more palatable to give a second thought to something more personal.

"And lo, the angel of the Lord of all heavens and all earths and all creatures, regardless of their planetary origin and biological classification, came upon them...And the angel said unto them, Fear not: for, behold, I bring you good tidings of great joy, which shall be to all sentient beings, whether biological or mechanical. For unto you is born this day in the Earth-designated ancient city of King David, also known as Bethlehem, a Saviour born on Earth, but not limited in power to a single world, which is Christ the Lord...And suddenly, there was with the angel a multitude of the heavenly host sent from a celestial realm that does not claim any specific planetary origin, praising God and saying, 'Glory to

God in the highest, and on all planets, stations, ships, and other dwelling-places of sentient beings, peace, good will toward sentients regardless of race, ethnicity, language, national origin, planetary affiliation...'"

There was no gold, frankincense, or myrrh the next morning. He wondered what the wise men would have brought if they had been limited to the ship-wide barter system that was the hallmark of every holiday season. And just where would the angel of the Lord have appeared in the absence of fields for shepherds to abide in?

Whatever the answers to those particulars were, he was certain that the good tidings of great joy had been for all people, no matter how many miles there were between "all people" and the little town of Bethlehem.

Santa Claus is Coming to Titan

Scott Ashby

nd baby Jana will never even know who Santa is, because we'll all be grown-ups by the time we move back to Earth."

"Trust me, Caro," Sulyn said, "Santa will be here on time, don't you worry about it."

"But we don't have a chimney, Mama, or even a fireplace," Caro wailed, "And everybody knows Santa only comes to your house down the chimney."

Sulyn sighed. Seven-year-old Caro had been fixated on Santa not making it to their new home on Titan ever since the community Thanksgiving dinner. She didn't have the heart to tell Caro the truth about Santa, not now, and destroy her child's faith in him. She'd already lost her home, friends, school, and everything else important to a child, including her puppy. Losing Santa would, Sulyn thought, be one loss too many.

At the same time, she was sick and tired of the constant whining.

"You know, there are lots of homes back on Earth without

fireplaces and chimneys, and Santa manages just fine there. And if you don't stop whining about it, he won't be leaving anything for you, whether or not he makes it all the way to Titan."

Caro clapped both hands over her mouth and dashed off into the tiny bedroom she shared with her eighteen-month-old sister.

Two days later, Caro was back at it, worrying her unnecessary worry again.

"Papa," Caro said at the dinner table, "is it true that nothing can get through the dome?"

Sulyn instantly knew this was another plea in the Santa department, but as most of the discussion had taken place while he was at work, her husband Rolf was unaware of the trap being laid by their crafty offspring.

"That's right, sweetie. Even though the dome is transparent, it's made of some of the strongest stuff known to mankind. It's completely safe."

Caro became visibly agitated. "So, if nothing can get through the dome, then how is Santa going to bring us our Christmas presents?" Her voice was pleading and dramatically traumatic, but there was also a hint of the triumph that she was proving her point about Santa.

The look on her husband's face as he realized he'd been outmaneuvered was classic. Sulyn wondered how he'd deal with the conundrum.

"Oh, well, if you're worried about Santa, don't be. He'll use the air lock, just like we did when we first got here. It's how he does it every year."

"But isn't it hard enough for him to take care of all the kids on Earth in one night? It took us ages to get here. There's no way!"

Rolf smiled at her.

"Well, there's a lot of people who say it's not possible for him to visit all the children on earth in one night, either, even if you take into account that he actually has a full twenty-four hours to make the deliveries, because the rotation of the earth makes it dark over the planet for the full rotation – a little more, if you consider that he can start in some places as soon as the sun goes down and the children go to bed on the 24th, and he has until the children start waking up on the 25th."

"But – "

"Eat your dinner before it gets cold," Sulyn interrupted.

That night, she spoke to Rolf about Caro's obsession with Santa.

"It's all she thinks about, night and day," she said, "and I'm having these arguments every other day.

"I don't want to tell her, but at the same time, I'm really tempted, just to get her to shut up."

Rolf put his arms around Sulyn. "It'll be all right. It's only three weeks until Christmas, and she'll find out Santa can make it here. Maybe seeing him at the party tomorrow night will help."

"I hope so." Sulyn sighed. "It's just so hard; her obsession is wearing both of us down."

"Hang on, love, I'm sure things will turn out all right." Rolf gave her an extra squeeze, meant to reassure, and they both went to bed.

Much to her disgust, Caro's obsession with Santa had become Sulyn's obsession with Caro's obsession, and she lay awake all night, thinking about what she was going to do about her daughter, and trying not to wake her husband with her restless body.

Next morning, as soon as the children had gone off to school, she called the community mental health officer and asked if she could see her before the children were out of school. Sulyn was told she could come now, and within ten minutes, she'd walked deep into the medical section of the dome and was sitting across a nice coffee table laden with an old-fashioned tea service. She nibbled on a scone while telling the woman, Debra, about Caro's problems and how they'd become her own.

"Well, of course, you know that every child in the colony has a package in Stores that will be delivered to your door Christmas Eve," Debra said, "but I agree with you that the presents themselves aren't really the problem here."

"They're not – we have some Christmas things too, some of them from us, others destined to be from Santa. Her problem is more about whether Santa can get here in time, and that he can't get in due to the lack of chimney and the impermeability of the dome."

"It's most likely a loss of control in her life that's triggered it. She had no choice about coming to Titan with you, and, as you noted, she's lost everything a child values in order to come…including her sense of belonging in a place. Are the other children accepting her at school? Any trouble there?"

Sulyn shook her head. "She hasn't said anything about the other children, but she has complained that the work itself was boring. She was in a gifted program back h – back on Earth."

Debra smiled. "You can say 'back home,' since that's how it feels to you. See, you have also lost everything familiar to you in this move. Dome living takes some getting used to, and you're also missing your friends, family, and home, the same as Caro, which is part of what irritates you when she starts whining. It's because you're a grown-up, and you feel like you're not allowed to whine."

Sulyn chuckled. "Well, but the job here is so lucrative, and seemed like a wonderful opportunity…"

"It is a wonderful opportunity, but I wonder about the cost in human sacrifice to every worker, particularly those who plan to go home. It's not just the twenty years here that you lose, you know…it's the forty years in cold-sleep each way, too. By the time you get back to Earth, it will have been a hundred years, and everything will have changed. You've permanently lost all of your friends, family ties, everything."

"I suspect the things the company stored for us will still be there, but we'll have forgotten why we thought they were important, won't we?"

"Quite likely. Although you might forge new relationships with your siblings' grandchildren, it won't be the same sort of relationship as if they'd grown up knowing you. I think part of you recognizes this, on an intellectual level, which is why your daughter's whining is all the more irritating; she's able to say what you aren't ready to face," Debra said. It sounded as though she'd said this a million times, which of course, she probably had.

Sulyn found it difficult to wrap her head around the fact that her parents had likely died of old age while she slept her way through the forty years that had seemed like only a few weeks of spaceflight.

"I'm sure you're right, Debra, but it's still three weeks in real-time to Christmas. How am I going to handle Caro until then?"

"Does she have any close friends at school? Perhaps playing with them and finding out naturally that Santa makes it to Titan every year will help. You could have a word with their mothers when you arrange the playdates. You could also see her teacher about a placement in a gifted group, or maybe even just moving her up a grade might help. In the meantime, try to be patient with her, do *not* tell her that Santa is simply handled by the parents, but be firm in not engaging in the discussion.

"And don't worry; it's not really an obsession, it's just her way of handling her concerns and making her own transition to living on Titan. She'll adjust just fine and might not even want to go back when your contract is up."

Fear clutched at Sulyn's heart.

"What will happen to our family if she doesn't want to go home?"

Debra winked. "Possibly nothing. Have you considered that you and your husband might also not want to go back?"

All the way home, Sulyn pondered the question that they might not want to go home. After twenty years, Earth's gravity would be oppressive. Baby Jana – and any other children born here – would probably have a particularly difficult time dealing with a gravity some seven times heavier than they'd grown up and learned to walk in, and even the three of them who remembered living on Earth would have a hard time adjusting.

Sulyn left a message for Caro's teacher to call her, preferably after bedtime, so Caro couldn't overhear the call.

That evening, she chatted with Caro's second-grade teacher, Tabitha Winsome, and discovered that Caro hadn't really made any close friends, partly because she was on a different level of both intelligence and education. Tabitha agreed they should do some testing and get Caro into a class where she would fit better, academically. Additionally, Tabitha said she had an idea about how to handle the Santa problem. Sulyn couldn't wait until Caro came home from school on Monday.

Caro danced in through the door after school, happy as a clam.

"What did you learn in school today?" Sulyn asked, as she did every day.

Caro looked smug. "I learned a secret."

"What was the secret about?" Sulyn pressed, though she thought she knew.

Caro shook her head. "It's a secret. If I tell you, then it isn't a secret anymore." She bounced off to her bedroom to play.

Sulyn wrote a short note to Caro's teacher. 'She's smug and won't tell me the "secret" she learned today. How am I going to be on the same page, if I don't know what you told her?'

A note came back swiftly. 'All I said was that I was going to tell them Santa's secret of how he gets to all the homes of all the well-behaved girls and boys, all over the galaxy, all in one night. That Santa needed to trust they wouldn't tell his secret. That he has power to travel through time – the sleigh is a time machine – and he's working all year, travelling everywhere, but because he can travel through time, it's always Christmas Eve when he pops out to deliver the presents."

Sulyn laughed. Why hadn't she thought of something that

simple? It certainly had seemed to work. Caro was being her usual, well-behaved self.

On Christmas morning, Caro opened her presents, both the ones from Santa, and those from her parents. She hugged Sulyn tight and said that she was sorry for all the yelling she'd done, and that she understood that only Miss Winsome had had permission to tell Santa's secret.

A Visit From NK-LAS

Kaki Olsen

was the shift before Christmas and on every deck,
Not a crewman was stirring. Believe me. I checked.
The crates were all stacked near the main supply room

In hopes that restock bots would fill them quite soon.
The helmsmen were nestled all snug in their berths
While dreams of new shortcuts they dreamed with great mirth.
The cap' at his station and I, new on shift,
Had taken our posts and both let our minds drift.
When on the ship's comm there arose such a rumpus,
I surveilled the decks lest some intruder trump us.
Without hesitation, I brought up the camscreen,
Dialed up resolution for what could be seen.
The lamps on the ceiling providing dim glow,
Gave some indication of what lurked below.
When a shape that detection could never avoid
Came into clear view; a resupply 'droid
With an old-fashioned mainframe so plodding and patient

A Visit From NK-LAS

I knew it was NK-LAS. That robot was ancient.
He directed the work – eight delivery drones came--
And he twittered and whistled and called them by name:
"Now, Foodstuffs! Now, Clothing! Now Gadgets and Cables!
On, Hygiene! On, Medicals! On, Leisure! On, Tables!
To the officers'quarters! To the exercise court!
Now go and deliver! Our time's running short!"
As O2 that flows in each room and mess hall
Without notice or bother between every wall;
So at every station the gift drones proved handy
With bins of things needed and even some candy.
And quite unexpected, I heard at my door
The scraping of a metal foot on the floor.
I turned from my screen in anticipation.
The door slid open; NK-LAS came to my station.
His parts begged an upgrade; his plating was tarnished;
But his midnight salute was with duty ungarnished.
A pack of materiel he held in his hand
And he seemed quite happy to fill each demand.
His optics – they winked! His posture upright!
I felt giddiness quite unexpected this night.
For this festive occasion, he'd donned a small bow
And a comic Santa hat – where from, I don't know.
Upon his arm plate he had painted a bell.
He wore a small wreath; he'd cleaned up pretty well.
He had a steel face with a sturdy construction
And usually arrived just in time for each function.
He was not inefficient – just like Santa's elf.
And I smiled when I saw him, in spite of myself.
As he set Christmas dinner onto a large plate,
I knew that great things come to those who will wait.

Kaki Olsen

He spoke not a sound, but served us right then.
By the end of the meal, we were both jolly men.
After laying out extras of our needful things
And moving with speed like creatures on wings,
He returned to his stock, to his drones gave a murmur,
And they flocked to his side, post-deliveries, with fervor.
But I heard him say ere he tramped out of sight –
"Happy Holidays, sirs, and to all a good night!"

The Nearly Lost Gift of the Magi

Scott Ashby

alorn snickered as he listened to the three main camels of the Magi's train talking together at the edge of the oasis. He'd always been able to understand the camels. Jalorn didn't advertise it because he didn't want a repeat of the punishment he'd received when he insisted to his father that he could understand them; hanging him upside down in his tent for the whole day as a lesson not to tell lies. The pesky flies buzzed around his face. The headache had been horrendous. And because he couldn't reach, Jalorn had developed an itch on his ankle. No matter how hard he'd wiggled, he hadn't been able to scratch it. Drove him nuts for hours.

That hadn't been the worst of it. Listening to the camels laugh about it was the nastiest part. They had snorted about it for weeks. Mac, the head Magi's camel started making Jalorn's life miserable by spitting the biggest, wettest, ickiest spit wads at him.

The other herdsmen didn't know about his gift. Not even the camels realized he could understand them. Jalorn shivered in the early morning chill. Even on Magi-3 it was cold until the edge of the sun reached them.

On the other hand, it was blazing hot on the side that faced the White Spiral Galaxy. That's why their tribe lived just at the edge of The Darkness and why they moved their village often to stay in the temperate zone as their planet slowly rotated.

The narrow strip of land they inhabited was between two great North and South mountain ranges. They got enough light to have daylight on a regular basis. There was water at each oasis to fill their needs. They had sun each day to grow their crops but not so much that it burned the plants up. Life was generally good.

Most of his tribe didn't believe in the Great Star theory. The idea that one day their star would become a brilliant light in the heavens of the White Spiral Galaxy until it burned itself out was considered ludicrous. How would anyone know something like that would happen, anyway?

Not everyone believed that the Son of the Universe had stayed here, being schooled in gathering all knowledge while waiting to be born onto a distant planet, either. Jalorn had secretly hoped that rumor was true. He so wished he could have met the Son of the Universe. The rumor also testified that the Son was kind and patient with everyone, no matter what.

Jalorn believed their star had been chosen by Father Universe for a special reason and for a great purpose and maybe Jalorn could be a small part of whatever it was. He prayed it would be so. That thought always gave him hope on the bad days when he was being picked on by the other herdsmen because of his small stature, or when the camels were being particularly beastly to him.

Last night, when he'd corralled them, he'd had to smack Mac on the backside rather hard to get him to move into the enclosure. By what Mac was now telling Turgus, his deputy camel, Jalorn knew there was a huge spitball with his name on it that would soon be hurtling in his direction.

Turgus was urging Mac to aim it at Jalorn's entire face while Roshut, the third Magi King's camel, was lobbying for a shot into Jalorn's ear. Jalorn shivered.

That evening, while Jalorn was settling the camels in the enclosure, he caught Turgus and Roshut having a quiet discussion. Well, for camels it was quiet. It sounded more like groans than their usual coughs, wheezes, and trumpeting.

"My master said he was gathering the gifts we have to carry to the manger to give to the earthly parents of the Son of the Universe because it was nearly time for his birth," Turgus said.

"What are we carrying?" Roshut asked.

"Some amount of gold, some myrrh, and some frankincense," Turgus answered.

Roshut choked on a ball of saliva before he could get his words together. "Myrrh! That's expensive! It's more costly than the other gifts put together!"

Turgus snorted his discontent. "And gold is heavy, and who's going to have to carry it? Not the Magi King, that's for sure!"

Mac was going to be carrying the myrrh for the head Magi King. Turgus would be left to carry the frankincense, which was further down the scale in value.

Roshut kicked out at Turgus' leg. "At least you have something more valuable than just a load of heavy, crummy gold. That's not worth a pile of camel dung these days," he said and spat a wad at the ground near Turgus' feet.

Turgus jumped aside to dodge the gooey mass of slop. "Hey, watch it! I don't need your slime on my foot. Save it for that worthless Jalorn. He's the one who slapped Mac on the rump and made Mac surly."

"Sorry, Turgus. So tell me what we're going to do to put a rock under Mac's foot so we don't have to listen to him lording it over us that he's got the best master, the most expensive saddle, and the costliest of the gifts for the birth of the Son of the Universe?"

"When we're on the trail, I'm going to steal the myrrh from him and, when it comes up missing, he won't be able to rub our faces in the fact that he was carrying the most important gift of all. That should keep him quiet for a solid month. In fact, it may lose him the position of being head camel to the main Magi King. I mean, if he can't be trusted to carry the most prodigious gift for the Magi King, what good is he?"

"I'm with you on this, Turgus. The last time he carried the best cargo, he didn't stop trumpeting for a whole sun cycle. I can't handle how long he'd be tooting his horn about this. How are you going to get it from him?"

"I haven't worked out all the details yet, but I'll call on you when I need your help. I promise you that. Maybe you can distract him so I can get at his pack. I'll let you know. In the meantime, keep it under your hump."

The camels moved off to join the others at the edge of the enclosure to settle down for the night.

Jalorn was thinking hard. He knew it was getting close to the time when the camel train would be transported down to the planet that the Son of the Universe would enter. All the herdsmen were busy polishing the leather and metal of the saddles and making the woven trappings as bright as a new coin.

He'd been working on a new blanket for his master's camel for months. That was the one thing he did that had earned him the spot to go with this caravan--his weaving was the best in the camp.

What if he got to the pack before the camels did and took the myrrh? Because he wasn't the one that cared for Mac, he wouldn't be blamed for the loss of the package. But if he was the one who found it, maybe then the other herdsmen would treat him with a little more respect. It might be worth the risk.

His dad was nervous to let him go on this journey. That was unusual. Normally, the man couldn't wait for him to be away from the village. He disliked the taunting mockery that came his way because of his son's shortness of stature. But this time was different. His dad was really worried about something.

So was Jalorn's mom. She'd given him a new shirt to wear. She'd made it herself. He looked good in it, too. It actually fit because it wasn't a hand-me-down from his cousins.

The next day, Jalorn carefully packed his kit. Dad spent the morning talking to him about what was expected of him. Mom spent the day telling him he was her special son, her own divine child, her precious little man. She told him of her love and how proud she was that he'd been chosen to go on The Crusade because of his weaving and his knowledge of camels.

Everything was at last ready. They would be leaving in the morning. Jalorn was quiet, watching for the chance to take the myrrh and hide it elsewhere in the baggage of the train.

He'd made a special place to house and hide it. All he had to do now was to wait until the camels were asleep and slip in to make the switch.

The camp quieted, and Jalorn knew this was his chance. He crept from his bedroll, quietly heading for the train's pile of luggage. It was just waiting to be loaded onto the camels an hour before dawn.

He reached down to open the pack holding the myrrh, when a small noise alerted him that he wasn't alone. He turned his head to look behind him.

A strange man was sitting on one of the packs, a most beautiful smile on his kindly face, warm and welcoming. He nodded at Jalorn and called him by name.

Jalorn sucked in his breath, unable to move. He was unable to look away from the kind man's face.

"Jalorn, please rethink this. Think how it would be for the Magi if, when they reach in their pack to give the gift to the Son of the Universe it wasn't there."

"How did you know..." Jalorn's voice trailed off.

"I know your heart, Jalorn. You're not a mischief-maker. You are usually kind and thoughtful. I know you don't talk back to the other herdsmen when they say unkind things to you. You don't even retaliate when the camels deliberately kick you or spit on you."

"But I want respect from both of them," Jalorn said quietly.

"I know you do. Let it be enough that I respect you. It doesn't matter what the others think. I value you and my Father values you. That's all that matters. Tomorrow I come into the worlds, and shortly the gifts of the Magi will be presented with honor and grace, and you and I will know it is by your choice that it could happen."

Jalorn looked at his hands for a few moments and felt like this kind stranger was more important than all the herdsmen and all the camels in the Universe. He decided to obey his advice.

He looked up, but the stranger had gone. Well, it didn't matter. He'd see the myrrh didn't go missing. It was, as the stranger had said, the right thing to do.

Jalorn went back to his bedroll, knowing his promise to obey was more important than gaining the respect of the other herdsmen and the camels. He had the friendship and respect of the Son of the Universe, who would be coming into the worlds tomorrow, and that was enough for him.

I'll Be On-Station for Christmas

Kaki Olsen

It was unusual for incoming ships to route personal calls to Waypoint Station weeks in advance, but it was four days after the Embarkation Day festivities when Sarah Vanderkamp was paged home to take a long-range communication.

"We have no Family Services here," her caller said after a few pleasantries were exchanged. "We haven't needed them, thank goodness, but things have gotten bad."

There were rumors of just how bad. The ship was coming in with a severe depletion of their medical supplies and registering a significantly lower number of passengers than the manifest had indicated upon launch.

"What can I do to help?"

"Give us options."

The request was a simple one that she heard daily, but it gave her license to get creative and that made her smile. "I'll be in touch."

Nathaniel had taken charge of dinner in case the call ran long, and she found Joseph setting the table while his dad finished seasoning the soup.

"How bad is it?" Nathaniel asked.

"It's about the *Excelsior,*" she answered.

That name was enough to bring a grimace to his face. In addition to the request for medical supplies and the change in passenger manifest, chaplains had been warned that they might need to preside over funerals of various traditions and belief systems and caskets had been donated by the station's mortuary for whatever was needed. The disease that had spread through the ship had been contained, but the onboard doctors believed that more deaths would be recorded because of the long-term effects and they had already requested that Waypoint Station evaluate all active cases to see if any of the patients could be saved by more advanced medical facilities. The men and women working on the *Excelsior* were competent and dedicated, but their best efforts couldn't hold up under the onslaught of a plague.

"A girl about Julia's age lost one parent to the disease a month ago and she lost the other to a cardiac arrest tonight," Sarah reported at a low enough volume so that Joseph would not overhear. "She has no other family on the ship to take her in and their ship's counselor asked me to officially step in."

"And they arrive in..."

"Sixteen days." The blessing of being here was that she not only had options to explore, but a staff of fifteen to take care of any other matters that might arise while she was working on a miracle. "I want them to dock with a long list of possible ways to find her a home."

No one had ever assigned the station's small group of

children to the welcome committee, but no one had the heart to stop them. Sarah knew that Joseph was the most likely to explain school rules to new students and Jonah would come home having befriended more than half of them without much effort. Julia would try to befriend the other half.

Devi Chaudhury called an hour after the *Excelsior* docked, frantic that Silva Noelle had been registered at customs while she was still on her way and there was no sign of the orphan now.

"She's on Deck 34 with my daughter," Sarah answered after a quick consultation of the elevator logs. They were officially meant for gathering traffic data, but the customs agents also gave all incoming passengers chits that would allow them to travel the station and access their ration credits at vendor stalls. Those chits also made tracking someone's movements relatively easy. "How about you meet them there?"

Devi checked in thirteen minutes later to say that Silva and Julia had politely thanked her for checking in on them and promised to have Silva back on board by dark.

By the time Julia and Silva temporarily parted ways, Sarah had been called into a Station Council meeting. She stopped at home to check on the kids and explain her upcoming absence, then quickly devoured a protein bar on the way to the conference center.

In an emergency, a full quorum of the Council was needed, but today, she found herself faced with Stationmaster Reginald Dunstan and Ada Fawkes from the legal office.

"Thank you for coming," Dunstan began. "I was hoping for an update from each of you on the matter of Silva Noelle."

"None of the families currently on board have expressed

interest in adopting her," Ada responded. "With the crisis in such recent memory, it's understandable that they are protecting their own before looking after someone else's concerns."

"Understandable, but disappointing," Sarah interjected, turning her attention to Dunstan. "Counselor Shumway has been looking after her, but Shumway is part of the crew instead of the colony. As I understand it, Silva is legally bound to those forming the colony, so it would require a transfer of citizenship for her to remain on the ship when it returns to Earth."

"I could make the legal arrangements for that transfer," Ada offered, "but she should have some say in the matter before the ship is clear for departure."

Silva was a minor, but she would be fourteen when they arrived and legally old enough to have a voice in her path forward. That was five thousand decisions and five years in the future, though, and there were more immediate concerns to address.

"None of the families on board will take her into their home," Ada said, "so what of the applicants here?"

Sarah immediately called up the files she had been compiling since that first conversation sixteen days ago. "Several of them are hesitant to foster a child of her age as it will be a complicated transition," she responded bluntly. "Two of them are unwilling to take someone in from off-station. Of the three that expressed interest in what we might classify a 'sky baby,' only one is immediately able to take her in."

"Which family?"

"Morin." Sarah had met them during the registration process but knew them better through her husband. Regina Morin also worked in Engineering, while Sean was in robotics. "The primary challenge there is that they have expressed interest in joining the crew of the *Excelsior* to cover for the crewmen who were lost on the way here. Before we can decide if they can make her a part of the family, we should let her decide if returning to the ship is what she wants."

It would be hard to give her an unbiased opinion on the matter, but they needed to start somewhere.

Customs cleared Silva for entry at 0931 the following morning, but Sarah had been waiting just beyond the checkpoint for five minutes by that time. She recognized the dark-haired girl from her identification file, but she was also drawing attention as someone who appeared hopeful that she wouldn't be noticed.

"Silva?"

The girl immediately froze in her tracks and gave her a wary look as Sarah approached and extended a hand. "I'm Julia's mom, Mrs. Vanderkamp. She's told me a lot about you."

The wary expression didn't vanish, but Silva accepted the greeting. "Where's Julia?"

"In school, but I hope you didn't think we forgot about you."

Silva's grip immediately tightened on the small chit "They said I was free to go where I wanted."

That wasn't technically true; her chit wouldn't allow her into private offices or beyond the entry to the warehouse levels and she certainly couldn't take up residence anywhere without a housing assignment, but those were guidelines that no nine-year-old needed to know.

"You're free to explore," Sarah clarified. "You've seen a lot of the station, but you haven't seen much of what it's like to live here. Would you like that?"

Her only answer was a curt nod, but at least Silva's fist relaxed a little. "What's first?"

"All the wonders of Waypoint Station and you took her to the library?" Nathaniel asked dubiously.

"Among other things," Sarah said with a chuckle. "I taught her how to use an information kiosk on the market levels and she helped me get groceries for tonight. I couldn't sneak her into Julia's P.E. Class, but I introduced her to one of the teachers and showed her the farms."

"And in return?"

"I let her show me her home."

It had been a sobering thing to see a passenger compartment filled with the remnants of a family's life. No one had processed the Noelles' personal effects, but Silva had packed all of her belongings into two suitcases as if she were expecting to be thrown out of her own home without any warning. She had plenty of supplies ranging from MREs to food cooked by others on the ship, but it was a lonely existence, nonetheless.

"If she stays onboard, she needs to feel safe making a home there again," Sarah had informed her staff, "and that's why I hope she'll stay here."

"What about the Morins?"

"They're still undecided," she said. "We have more than enough volunteers like them for crew positions and the discussion *should* include any person they might bring into the family."

Sarah had just set the meeting for the next evening when she had a call from Deck 34. She arrived to find Nicholas setting out bed linens and considering the merits of two types of pillows.

"Who's moving in?"

"That remains to be seen," he said cryptically. "A girl of my acquaintance is staying overnight so she can participate in a school day tomorrow and I hope to make her comfortable."

"I appreciate that," Sarah replied. "Why did you call *me* here?"

"A girl of my acquaintance is staying overnight," he echoed himself. "I understand that she's your acquaintance."

"She's under my stewardship," Sarah corrected. "I'm trying to find a balance what will make her happy and yet will give her a home. So far, I feel as though I'm missing the mark."

"I think all parents feel that way." He returned one of the pillows to the crate and turned a sympathetic smile in her direction. "You've enlisted the help of wonderful people, though, and I think she could be very happy here."

"That's not my choice to make."

His eyebrows raised in disbelief that she would make such an erroneous assumption. "It's not your choice to make alone, you mean to say," he corrected her.

The Vanderkamps had never considered taking in a sky baby, but the vote was unanimous in favor of adding to their family. Jonah began planning what games he would teach her. Joseph made an enthusiastic trip to Deck 34 for everything from a bed to school supplies. Nathaniel and Sarah split the duties of school enrollment and legal guardianship.

The meeting went ahead on December 23 as planned, but without the attendance of the Morins.

"We have decided to approve your request to stay," Stationmaster Dunstan announced with the self-satisfied smile of Santa removing a large present from his sack. "As long as you wish it, Waypoint Station can be your home."

Silva blushed with relief but looked to Sarah for more good news. "So I need to find someone to let me stay with them now?"

"I'm working on it," she answered with a sly wink at her superior.

They toasted her new citizenship in the family quarters with all their favorite recipes. Julia bemoaned the fact that they'd *just* finished classes until the new year, but said she'd catch her up every day of vacation when they weren't exploring.

It was after the dishes were dried and they'd obliged Jonah with a board game that Silva nervously said she'd probably better go back to the guest room.

"That's the thing," Nathaniel said. "If you'd like, we have your room ready for you to stay here for as long as you want."

It didn't take much persuasion for Silva Noelle to come home for Christmas.

O Tannin Bomb

Scott Ashby

t was a beautiful spring morning and Douglas Firendon maneuvered his walking-roots through the top six inches of the forest floor, letting the fallen needles and minor rocks slide beneath and between his smaller rootlets. After all, you couldn't get any nourishment from rocks, and only a small amount of nitrogen from the dead and fallen needles. The rich mulch of the fallen deciduous leaves had a lot better flavor.

He paused on his way and stripped a couple of thin branches from a tea bush, then continued to the small pool where he dropped the branches into the water. After a time, some of the pool's water had turned brown around the tea-bush branches, and Doug slid his feeder roots into the brown water.

Many of his friends thought he was crazy, but he'd really come to like the taste of the tea he made each morning. The tannins were delicious and had an extra effect of helping him wake all the way up and stay awake through his classes. He only wished he had time to make tea during the day, as well, but young trees generally rooted at night, and feeding didn't interfere with their daily occupations, so none of the adult trees felt there was any need of nourishment breaks. As they were officially classified as plants – sentient plants, to be sure, but plants nonetheless-- they simply didn't need nutrients as much – or as often – as the animals.

His mother kept telling him the tea was the cause of his pollen problems, but he disregarded her advice. After all, none of his friends were tea-drinkers, but several of them also had pollen problems. It was just a part of adolescence, the school nurse had informed him, and advised him to forget about it – eventually, as he matured, he'd stop having the pollen attacks.

They weren't too bad, really, Doug reflected. He'd get a sudden itchy sensation, then he'd quiver all over, and everything around him would be coated in slightly sticky, bright yellow pollen.

When he'd grown out of this, he'd only make the pollen every spring, shed it within a couple of weeks, and be done with it for the rest of the year.

In late autumn, the guardians chose where they would sleep for the winter. Doug wasn't tired, but he knew it was time, so he chose a somewhat protected place and settled his rootlets in for the winter.

Not all trees moved about, of course, in fact most of them didn't, but there were always a few of each generation who were the shepherds, the guardians, who moved about and gathered news for the trees who didn't move. Doug was glad he'd ended up with the extra gene that allowed him movement, even though he had to protect himself and the other shepherds from the knowledge of the beings that called themselves huumons.

Doug wasn't certain what brought him to full alert, but something wasn't quite right in his part of the firry forest. He'd been almost asleep, darn it, and now it would take him another month or so to truly settle into sleep. He shook the snow from his limbs in preparation to move.

A huumon voice pipped, and within seconds, five more huumons had surrounded Doug, who was not permitted to move in their presence. They dug Doug's roots from the earth and placed him into a large square container. The huumons severed several of his roots as they dug, which caused no small amount of pain, even in Doug's semi-somnolent winterized state. He hastened healing juices to the ends of the affected roots to seal them off, to deal with the pain as well as protect him from infection.

Once they'd crammed him in the container, they shoveled a little dirt over his roots, though it wasn't nearly enough to gain any nutrition from. Then the huumons heaved the box onto something large and flat, and strapped the box down. They left him there for a long time, returning to place other boxes on the flat surface, but the other boxes here contained only trees, no other guardians. The huumons all climbed into a pod at one end of the flat surface.

A loud, rumbling noise filled the forest, then Doug realized why the boxes had been strapped down. The flat surface began to move, going faster and faster – more speed than Doug had ever experienced. It was dark and he couldn't see where he was going, he was moving too fast. As a guardian, he also experienced the fear of the trees around him. He did his best to comfort them, but really didn't know what he could say to them without lying; after all, he didn't know what was happening either.

They moved out of the forest and were surrounded by the huumons surrogate caves. The further they went, the harder it became to breathe. The air tasted foul, and although there was plenty of carbon dioxide, there were other chemicals that blocked his stomata and made it difficult to take the carbon dioxide in.

The artificial caves grew larger, and the flat surface slowed, then stopped. The huumons got out of the front and busied themselves with unstrapping the boxes and moving the trees through an opening and into the artificial cave. Doug's was the last box they moved.

The huumons moved his box through the artificial cave's opening and through a goodly-sized tunnel, then into a vast room filled with trees in boxes. Had he been moving under his own power, he would have stopped short at the sight of so many trees in boxes inside an artificial cavern.

It was light in the cavern, but the light brought no nutrients such as natural sunlight provided. Apparently the huumons had created an artificial sun to lighten their artificial cavern.

The huumons set his box down, then moved around the room putting the most horribly contaminated water Doug had ever tasted into all the trees' boxes. Then the huumons all left. As the last one exited, all the light disappeared.

The trees whispered to each other in the darkness; it sounded like small breezes rustling the leaves of aspens. As

Doug listened, he realized he was the only guardian in this artificial cave, and that all the trees were of varying sorts of evergreens – not a single deciduous tree in the cavern. With no answers to any of their questions, it didn't take long for the trees to settle into silence for what remained of the night.

During the darkness, Doug felt the familiar itching, then the puff that meant he'd had another pollen attack. He shrugged to himself. It wasn't like there was anything he could do about it.

The artificial suns snapped on, flickering into brightness. Many huumons came bustling into the cavern and set to work. Slowly, Doug figured out the pattern. The huumons first touched the soil in the boxes and put more of the nasty water on some of the trees. When they came to his box, the huumons seemed dismayed at his pollen attack. They stood on guard around the base of his box, and the several other boxes he'd accidentally covered with the pollen. Despite the stickiness, they cleaned up every last speck of it.

The huumons split into groups of four and each group worked together on one tree at a time. First, they wrapped some substance around the boxes the trees were in. Then, balancing carefully on the edges of the boxes, they wrapped each tree in thin vines that they connected to other vines laying on the floor. They wrapped each tree again in glittery vines, then hung different things on many of the branches of each tree. The huumons always made sure that the very top of each tree was cut off and then adorned. Finally, a single huumon came past and hammered on the corner of each tree's box. When that one came to Doug's box, he could see she was attaching what looked like a leaf on a small vine to his box. There were some black marks on the leaf.

When all the trees had been adorned, the huumons left again, and the artificial suns were turned off. Recalling the huumons' irritation with his pollen outburst, Douglas spent most of the night gathering all his power into one huge burst of pollen. Some of the trees on the other side of the cavern coughed, and he knew he'd spread the pollen well. He was exhausted. He felt as though he might never pollinate again. At the same time, he was eagerly waiting to see the huumons' reaction. If he could annoy them enough, he might be taken home.

The artificial suns flicked back on, and everything Doug could see in every direction was covered with the sticky yellow pollen he'd released last night. He was already working on producing a burst for tonight, if it was needed.

The huumons seemed very upset, and they set about cleaning pollen immediately, but it had spread too far. They had what looked like a very angry meeting, with loud voices and wild waving of limbs. Some of them left for a period of time and returned with large rolls of what looked like artificial grass and laid it out in the aisles between the trees. In the meantime, others labored at re-wrapping the boxes the trees were in, while others saw to the adding of thc horrible water to the boxes where the scanty dirt had dried.

Before they were finished laying out the artificial grass (what was it with huumons that everything was fake?), Doug discovered what the thinner vines were for; there was a loud crack and a humming sound, and the thinner vines on every tree lit up in various colors. Some were all one color, but most were many colors. There were nature colors, like green and blue and yellow, but there were also colors Doug didn't have names for. Most of the trees' colors were steady, but some of them changed colors, and some of them flashed in different patterns. Doug's were all one color – the color of snow – and the other sparkly things hanging off his branches matched.

Lots of other huumons entered the cave, looking with delight at the decorated trees. Many of the people who walked past stopped to admire Doug; or maybe they were admiring his decorations. Some of the people looked at the brown leaf on the corner of his box, then shook their heads and walked on. Eventually, one of the huumons looked at his box leaf, then summoned another huumon, pointed at Doug, and handed over a quantity of green leaves. Doug wondered what that was about.

After a long time, there was another snap, and all the colored lights on the trees went out. Huumons came and grabbed Doug's box and dragged him toward the cavern's exit. The movement surprised him so much that he almost lost his pollen load all over the huumons, but he managed to hang on. It might be more helpful wherever they were taking him.

He was put on the flat thing again and taken to a different artificial cave, then lifted from his box and shoved into a hole in the ground. Wonderful, natural dirt was shoveled over what remained of his roots, and then snow was placed over the dirt. He wouldn't really be able to root until spring, when the earth thawed.

A long vine was brought over and attached to his thin vine, prompting the white lights to shine again, and he was left alone.

O Tannin Bomb

The wind was chilly, with no older trees to break it, but it was something he could live with. At least he was no longer in the surrogate cave with the artificial sun. He released his last bunch of pollen and tried to settle down to sleep again.

Away in a Mess Hall

Kaki Olsen

Note: This is clearly inspired by the wonderful tradition of Las Posadas in various countries. In it, children go from door to door for nine nights, seeking a place for the Holy Family to stay and there are specific responses as you will soon see.

It was amazing how much work went into a small celebration. It was easy to make a birthday cake or reserve the convocation hall on Deck 4 for a wedding reception. The schools hosted end-of-term parties at the gaming arcade or the sports compartments that were the highlight of Deck 5. The elaborate nature of each event depended on the income or trading skill of the organizer, so it took some planning to decide which occasions merited each year's splurges.

Las Posadas, though, were a community effort and this was especially true for the first holidays of the voyage. Christianity wasn't even the majority religion on *Seventh Dawn,* but the average age of the passengers on board was lower than the captain had ever seen before, so they decided it was important to make something special for the occasion.

The right fruits and spices for *ponche navideño* were reserved well in advance, but assignments were handed out to young and old in each of the three *barrios* on board for *masa* duty. Nine nights of tamales required a lot of *masa harina* and the time-consuming preparation was as joyful a gathering as anything else during the season. Even the candles carried in the procession were made over the year from beeswax collected at the carefully-tended beehives on Deck 2, and *piñatas* were enthusiastically made under strict supervision in classrooms.

There were objections, of course, but not along the usual lines.

"I'm not going to threaten violence," came the message from the head of security.

"Guilty until proven innocent," said Judge Clairborne. "I won't say, 'I cannot open. You may be a robber.' I respectfully decline."

"Medical ethics forbid me from turning away a patient," added the ship's superintendent of medicine.

"We don't have a donkey, but if it's accompanied by a member of the transportation authority, we can lend a hoversleigh," commented one of the ship's engineers.

Most of these were said with a wink, though it took some negotiation to convince Officer Polat that no one would actually be permitted to attack the pilgrims. He was simply hypervigilant when it came to such things.

Polat didn't have to worry about his moral dilemma on each of the first three nights, since Jose and Maria (Hector and Lupita) first went to the Housing Administrator. Hector's father worked for the transportation authority, so the hover-sleigh "donkey' was easily arranged. There was the custom-ary procession, but this included a larger percentage of the local population than usual. After all, it was something of an unwritten rule that no one ranked high enough to be rude to the ship's children and many people simply wanted to watch some of their fellow passengers break character.

Hector looked slightly nervous at the crowd following him at the first door, but his clear voice raised over the silent crowd.

> "In the name of heaven
> I request that you grant us shelter
> Given that she cannot walk
> She my beloved wife."

Administrator McManus was known to take emergency calls at all hours of the night and had once spent three days sleeping in his office so a family could escape their flooded cabin. He drew a laugh when he turned the Holy Family away with one particular chorus:

> "I don't care about your name.
> Let me go to sleep.
> Because, as I said,
> We shall not open."

Of course, he eventually yielded, but he struggled to keep a straight face when repeatedly asked for shelter and he had to be reminded more than once to not skip any verses.

On the second night, Father Raymundo was the one to

improbably ask, "If it's a queen who's asking for it, how is it that at night, she travels so alone?" He played his role with gruff good humor until the moment that he asked the procession to join in for the chorus:

"Let's sing with joy!
Everyone at the thought!
That Jesus, Joseph, and Mary
came today to honor us!"

His piñata was smaller than the others', but he had the most accurate headcount and had prepared the feast accordingly.

Lupita gave the innkeeper a hug first thing on the third night. They'd visited the oldest person on the ship and that happened to be her *abuela* Lupe.

She was the least convincing when saying, "Come in, pilgrims. I did not know you." The visitors sang with great enthusiasm when they entered: "May heaven swamp you with happiness."

Instead of expecting a feast at this shelter, the people in the procession brought the food with them and left Lupe and her namesake for a smaller celebration than usual.

The next night, Officer Polat answered with an unusually broad smile. He uttered the objectionable threat, but he was also the innkeeper to spend the most time welcoming the guests.

There was more apprehension when the procession approached the fifth night's host. Mr. Baker was a familiar sight to every parent and student on the ship, but there were rarely good reasons to go to his office.

"Joseph" had been called in just a few days before for disrespecting his math teacher. He had been given extra chores on that occasion, but that seemed to give him added courage when refusing to be turned away. Mr. Baker, for his part, was the most convincing when grumbling that "This is not an inn. Please continue ahead." By the end of the night, he granted a commutation of Hector's sentence and they parted on good terms.

On the sixth night, the doctor on duty played her part well. "Please leave the donkey here," she added when they began gathering for the feast.

"It's not a donkey," Lupita said very seriously.

"Well, not with that attitude," Dr. Jamison said, "but I can give him a checkup. I don't think he's feeling like a donkey at all."

Lupita gave her a confused look, but she apparently decided that the doctor would come to her senses soon and joined her friends for the *piñata*. Dr. Jamison attracted a crowd as soon as she tried to use her stethoscope on the donkey, but she eventually declared him to be in need a rest before the next night and otherwise in fine health.

The family who had most recently added a new member sang very quietly at the door on the seventh night and asked them to have *ponche* next door, where there wasn't a sleeping baby. Mary and Joseph insisted on leaving most of the feast on their table, but that had been agreed upon before the first night.

On the eighth night, the procession came to a very unusual place. Most people on board didn't have a reason to go to the command deck and even fewer came to the bridge. "Mary and Joseph" were so awestruck that it took some prompting for them to start singing *pedir posadas*. The captain was the first to turn them away, but the following verses were exchanged with the navigator, the communications, officer, and the pilot before the first officer welcomed them in.

Luckily, there were no course corrections needed for the next little while. The nativity was displayed on a sensor screen rather than being set up as it had in other "inns."

"Don't worry," Captain van Buren said by way of farewell, "I don't think you'll have any problem finding shelter tomorrow."

On the *Seventh Dawn*'s planet of origin, the last visit was often made to a church, but this *posada* ended on the ninth night at the mess hall.

All of the innkeepers were there to welcome them; even the family with a baby came for a few minutes. No one counted the numbers, but there were very few faces missing from the community.

The *ponche* seemed to never run out. The *piñatas* were done with extra care. Best of all, dozens of voices sang the responses, so that people far from the mess hall could hear the

Kaki Olsen

best wishes for the season:

"Come in, holy pilgrims!
Receive this corner!
Because, even though the place is poor,
I offer it to you from my heart!
Let's sing with joy!
Everyone at the thought!
That Jesus, Joseph, and Mary
Came today to honor us!"

Away in a Spaceship

Scott Ashby

uke's Law: The three most useless things in aviation are altitude above you, a runway behind you, and air in the fuel tanks.

Baxter's Law: The average general aviation fuel tank will outlast the average human bladder. Fill up the one every time you stop to empty the other.

Ancient laws, those, but nearly every bit as useful today as when my seventh-great-grandmother wrote them in the margins of her log. Particularly today, when I had ignored both, and neglected to refuel my ship when I'd stopped at station K-9-4-10 to stretch my legs, get some lunch, and, well, empty 'the other.' I thought I'd told station services I needed more fuel, and I surely recalled signing the credit chit, but the bare fact was that not twenty minutes ago I felt the shiver and heard the whoosh that signified the last of my fuel being expended. I had a bad case of air in the fuel tanks, and I was pretty sure it was terminal.

I checked my heading for what was, at least, the hundredth time since the fuel gave out. I had plotted a multiple-legged flight that involved boosting to a particular speed and then making no less than fifteen navigational burns. This was a particularly busy section of space to navigate, if you counted obstacles, rather than other ships, as busy; you either had to go way out and around, which took a lot longer, or you had to take the more direct, but also more complicated route, skirting around and through nebulae, globular clusters, and roving magnetic storms. It was nearly a month faster, which was why I preferred this trickier route. It kept me on my toes as a pilot, but it also allowed me to charge a premium rate for passengers and cargo that needed to get to The Junction faster. My usual clients were businessmen who were desperate to beat out their competition and were willing to pay extra to do so. There were probably only half a dozen other pilots who routinely used this route, and I hadn't seen any of them at station K-9-4-10.

I didn't have any passengers this time around, which was more usual than not, but I was full up on cargo that, along with myself, wasn't going to get to The Junction. Though the *Robin* was capable of drifting on its current heading until the end of time, I wasn't going to be keeping her company that long. I'd been in the middle of burn eight when the fuel had given out. While I was no longer on my original course, I was also not on my intended course for this leg, which meant anyone else foolish enough to take the short path between K-9-4-10 and The Junction wouldn't be passing by me, unless they did it in the next half hour or so.

When you also consider that fuel is not just used for propulsion, but for lights, heating, cooking, and oxygen recycling…well, even if the *Robin* was found, I probably would be starved, dehydrated, or frozen long before then. I'd put on several layers of thermal undies and was already feeling the cold. Not that I ever wasted a lot of fuel keeping the *Robin* comfortably warm.

Of course, I had turned on the distress beacon and recorded a mayday and set it on auto-repeat as soon as I'd felt the last of the fuel go – I like living, and I'd like to do a whole lot more of it. But I also knew the odds were stacked against me: no fuel, no heat, no navigation; in an area of space where magnetic storms would easily hide or erase my transmissions, and where very few ventured.

The radio crackled, and I reached out with a manual transmission. The radio kept crackling every few minutes, and I kept transmitting, hoping they were able to hear me, even though I couldn't hear them. The crackling continued on and off for at least ten minutes, though it felt like forever. Then finally, a voice came through, though only patchy.

"…That you…*Robin*…keep talkin'…can hardly hear…"

I kept talking, rambling on, not making much sense. If they were navigating to me by my voice transmission, I'd give them plenty of voice. I turned off all the systems I could, and lit up all my exterior lights, then boosted the power to the radio, doing everything I could to be noticed.

"I see you, *Robin*, hang on there." The voice was loud, clear (and therefore near) and unmistakably belonging to my biggest business rival, Oldfather.

Shortly, I heard the clang of our ships touching, then the buzzing of maintenance robots welding the ships together and attaching a flexi-lock.

I grabbed a couple of ship-suits and stuffed them into a carrisack, then went to the airlock. A flexi-lock is a plastic tunnel, held rigidly open with a long, spiral of wire. There's a knotted rope that runs down the middle of it, so you can pull yourself along hand-over-hand. It's larger in circumference than most airlock doors, and clamps magnetically to the sides of the two ships, making it possible to transfer from the airlock of one ship to the airlock of the other without having to suit up. Nice idea, so long as the spring-loaded spiral wire doesn't come undone while you're in it, or the thin plastic keeps all the air in. Passengers love them. I don't trust them.

I suited up, fastened the carrisack to my belt, passed through my airlock (closing both the interior and exterior doors securely behind me), and grabbed the rope, making my way to Oldfather's ship. He didn't meet me at the airlock, but had left a digi-message on the airlock keypad, inviting me to come on board, asking me to secure both airlock doors, and directing me to wait for him in the main passenger lounge, where he'd join me as soon as he could.

I took that to mean that he was busy directing the maintenance bots, getting both our ships back on course, and he'd deal with me later. I took off my suit and found an empty rack to stow it in, securing it properly. I know how to be a good guest and keep things tidy. In a ship running at no- or low-grav, you keep everything secured at all times and that's a good practice to observe even in a ship with full grav, because you don't want things floating around if the grav suddenly quits.

I followed the blinking green lights at the corner of the deck plate and the wall through the corridors to the passenger lounge. The corridors seemed to have only about 1/5 gravity, but I was an old hand in space, and could routinely deal with anything from zero to two Gs, and was certified to take up to a full seven, if horizontal and wearing the right equipment…though I wouldn't want to go much past three or four on a regular basis.

The door to the passenger lounge had the flashing yellow light of a gravity change on a pad next to it, and I paused long enough to read the warning. The lounge was being maintained at half-grav. Fair enough. I used the handle next to the door to pull myself to an upright position, then carefully stepped through the gravity interface, and managed to step into the lounge without falling on my face. I was sure Oldfather was at least recording in the lounge, if not actively watching, and I didn't want to give him anything to laugh at later. I know when I have unaccompanied passengers, I lock them into safer areas of the ship and record at all times, including 'freshers and cabins, just in case of liability issues – so I can prove truth if it gets into a he said/she said/it said thing.

It was three days before Oldfather appeared, though I was able to procure food, drink, and entertainment in the passenger lounge, and found a cabin with a private 'fresher that opened off the lounge for sleeping. I stayed in the lounge all during the days, because that's where he'd asked me to be. I prepared my own sustenance and cleaned up after myself, because I try to be a considerate guest. Given my quasi-cordial relationship with Oldfather, I was pretty sure that 'guest' wasn't exactly the right word to describe my status at the moment.

Oldfather sauntered into the passenger lounge like he owned the place and, let's face it, he did. "You making out okay?"

"Better than I was doing before you came along," I replied, trying for the same casual tone he'd used, as though I didn't owe him my life. "How much am I paying for room, board, and transport?" I hoped it wasn't more than my credit account, but I could probably work off an overdraft, if it was.

"Eight days' passage, standard rate."

I mentally sighed in relief. That was well within my budget.

"And standard salvage and cargo rates for your ship."

I swallowed. That would take everything I had, including what I'd get paid for the cargo I was carrying.

I punched a few buttons on my wristpad and named a figure that would still allow me to purchase fuel and food for my next trip.

Oldfather nodded. "That will do. Or…you could work it off. I've got a few errands I need run."

"Legal?"

He nodded, then added, "Legal, but discreet."

"How many errands?"

"One, really, but there are multiple stages. Passengers. Here, then there, then other places…and no questions asked."

I hesitated a long time; he was known for operating a little too close to the wind. "Okay, but I have the discretion to stop if a law is even going to be bent and pay you the sum I've already named. And you'll pay for fuel, commissary, and landing fees."

He agreed so swiftly that I wondered who I'd be ticking off by running his passengers around.

"When we get to The Junction, I'll have my bots unweld our ships. You need any repairs?"

I shook my head. "No, the *Robin*'s just out of fuel. For some reason, they didn't fill me to the top at K-9-4-10."

He smiled, and I knew. I'd never be able to prove it, but I knew he'd picked me to do his dirty work for him, to take these passengers around. I knew he'd been behind the fueling 'misunderstanding', so that he could rescue me, put me in his debt. And I knew that, somehow, these passengers he wanted me to haul, were going to change my life, and I'd be absorbed into his ring of associates, and I'd never be free of him.

At least I had my life.

I Heard the Engines on Christmas Day

Kaki Olsen

here was an old aphorism that you got what you paid for, but this wasn't supposed to be true of interplanetary travel.

"What's the station equivalent of highway robbery?"

Captain Washburn had been in this argument for an hour now and while she wasn't the most belligerent woman by nature, the official mechanics were about to get on her last nerve, and they knew it.

"It might be highway robbery if we were trying to charge you exorbitant amounts," Johanssen, the chief object of her irritation, responded.

It had all started with the crew insisting that there was only one way to repair the problem. Washburn wasn't an expert in such things, but ten years of making it to the next port of call under less-than-ideal circumstances had taught her that there was no such thing as a single remedy to a single problem. Johanssen apparently followed the same school of thought, but he was insisting on an approach that made life difficult for the good captain today.

"You're withholding parts that are public access according to the trade guidelines."

"Public access as long as the hosting station can spare them," he countered. "At the moment, that's not the case."

"You're telling me that this place will fall out of the sky if you help us?" she challenged.

"I'm saying I don't want six hundred people and two thousand bots to be crossing their fingers that we won't need those parts before the next resupply."

Johanssen attempted to look sympathetic, but it came off as smug. Washburn snatched her tablet back and stalked off without another word.

The crew was no less irritated with Johanssen when she explained the dead end, but they were more optimistic about the outcome.

"I've done some checking around," Zhao reported, "and there are two private vendors who can sell us what we need –"

"As long as we pay a price determined by these things being in high demand," Washburn told her usual mechanical know-it-all. "And I'm guessing none of them extends credit."

"We don't need them to," her first officer said. "We've got the payment for every passenger on this ship and we've got a grace period before we have to start reimbursing for unreasonable delays." At a look from her, Cameron sighed. "And we have two more scheduled stops, so we want to make sure we don't have to rely on that grace period this time around."

"Or come up short on funds when we need to do a more significant repair."

The main problem wasn't that they had malfunctioning engines. Smart drivers on Earth had spare tires for their cars and smart pilots could call on the sort of engines that NASA had used to get *Apollo 11* to the moon. But relying on more traditional rockets meant that you ran the risk of having equally old-fashioned mechanical problems. Spare tires weren't meant to be permanent solutions, just a way to get you to the nearest shop and it was very risky to assume that it could hold out that long. It would be unsafe and unethical to take even one person into space with only an emergency backup as the most reliable source of propulsion and she had thirty people waiting nervously for their itineraries. If they were delayed much longer, their passengers might even start talking about putting down roots here or transferring to a ship that had a few extra spots in the passenger section and the bank balance would go even lower than it already was.

"Did Johanssen have any other ideas?" Cameron asked.

"He suggested duct tape, spit, and a lot of prayer," Washburn muttered. "How many religions do we have represented, anyway?"

"We have two Christian missionaries, a rabbi, and at least six Muslims this time," Zhao said without needing to check; he was the people-watcher on the crew and was sort of famous for being able to recall the connections and details so they could call in favors. "I hadn't gotten around to the more personal questions with the rest of them."

"Zhao, get me the quotes for the parts from a few more people in case we get desperate. Cameron, see if you can find any of our allies on the list of ships arriving this week. I'm going to make some quiet inquiries about bartering or getting a loan from one of the outlier stations."

It might mean taking on cargo to deliver at their next stopping place, but there were much worse ways to get back into space than agreeing to haul rations or prefabricated housing units in exchange for a short-term rescue.

The quotes were ready before anything else, of course, and predictably depressing. Cameron had reached out to two captains and was waiting for a response, while three people at the nearby Horizon Station had sent back thanks-but-no-thanks messages.

Washburn wasn't much for organized religion, but she started to ask any higher power out there that they'd catch a break.

"I've got good news," Cameron announced two days later.

Washburn gestured her to the empty seat next to Zhao, but kept eating breakfast because 'good news' was a relative term. "Say the magic words," she instructed after swallowing her oatmeal.

"Salvage Sale," Cameron answered.

The words weren't exactly magic, but they definitely were worth further consideration. "Are you talking about the *Janus?*"

"We're the first ones to know," Cameron said. "I've been giving their engineers a helping hand and that means I was there when the captain decided it wasn't worth putting up a fight anymore. They're hitching a ride back to Terminus and selling the *Janus* for spare parts."

"That's great," Zhao said, "but…"

"I'm not finished."

Kaki Olsen

Cameron wasn't usually one to interrupt a ranking officer, so Washburn leaned forward in interest. Zhao, following her lead, remained silent.

"We've still got four berths available and they just stranded two passengers and a crewman."

"As long as they can pay, that shouldn't be a problem."

Cameron stayed further comment with an upraised finger. "We can take the contract transfer for the two people and they'll negotiate with us if we can take on the crew."

The two transfers would definitely help pay for the repairs, so even Zhao looked intrigued at the proposal. "What's the crewman's job?" he asked.

"Mechanic," Cameron said proudly. "If you approve of him, we could use an extra pair of hands and they'll have a personal interest in telling us the best parts to get us going again."

After a moment in which Zhao tried to avoid feeling territorial and Washburn found a schematic for the *Janus'* ship class, the mechanic nodded. "I can make the interview quite hands-on."

"I'm sending you the plans," Washburn said before attaching the file to a message. "I want to know before we set foot in the salvage yard what we could get out of it and what might still work if you need to get creative."

Zhao arched an eyebrow as if to say it was insulting to think he couldn't get creative on the fly. Washburn turned back to Cameron.

"Can you get a meeting with the passengers?"

"They can meet us for dinner," she said. "Captain Dent from the *Janus* has offered to make the introductions *and* pick up the check."

Under other circumstances, that would have made Dent seem suspiciously eager to get rid of passengers, but the *Janus* was past the contract-standard grace period and this was probably going to create credit problems for Dent for years to come.

"I'll take the meeting. You." She tilted her chin at Zhao. "See how eager this mechanic is to prove his worth."

The answer turned out to be "very" and Moises Orellano came to the interview with a plan that put Zhao's preliminary assessment to shame. There was nothing particularly outstanding about the passengers, but they didn't ask for any discounts or expect any special treatment.

The repairs started out promising, but there was some disgruntled mumbling between Zhao and Orellano that made Washburn leave them alone and check in with the quartermaster on Deck 34 instead.

Cameron looked pleased with herself in spite of parts that needed more fine-tuning than anticipated. Washburn decided not to discourage her, since the stroke of good luck had been at her hands.

First thing on Friday, though, Washburn found herself jolted awake by a slightly rattling hum that made her teeth chatter. Fifteen seconds later, the rattle ended with a lurching sensation.

And then, the vibration cut off all together. Alarmed, Washburn grabbed her slippers and headed for the door.

Cameron was nowhere to be found, but Zhao had made himself comfortable in the first officer's chair. Still bleary-eyed and disoriented, Washburn folded her arms. Zhao held up a hand for silence, but the next sound on the ship was a much more steady and familiar rumbling.

"Merry Christmas, Captain Washburn," he said. "I'd like to take a few laps, but if all goes well, we should be able to begin boarding in a few hours."

Because nothing could be perfect, it actually took six hours before the new dynamic duo was satisfied, but the passengers had to cancel their dinner plans that night to board their home for the next few weeks.

Instead of bidding farewell with the usual "Clear skies," Washburn signed off with "Peace on Waypoint, good will toward men."

One More Cryosleep 'Til Christmas

Kaki Olsen

his," Lieutenant Dujardin announced, "is the beauty of modern technology."

"That's what you say about everything from nutrient paste to the toilets," the expedition's lone civilian and cartographer, Mabel Evans commented. "The phrase is starting to lose its potency."

"Never," Dujardin said. "It's always true."

Four months into the flight, Commander Gervais knew that there was no arguing with him. He'd ostensibly been chosen for his leadership skills, but everyone in the command crew as well as the lower-ranking personnel all quickly realized that those skills included trying to instill a sense of awe in everyone else. It was enough to make them all wish he would marvel at the power of sedatives for a while at least once a week, but they also had many occasions to be grateful that things worked as well as they did.

"Don't be too hard on him," Gervais reminded them. "You were all asked to be prepared for this meeting and I'm not judging him for having enthusiasm as part of those preparations."

"I'm very enthusiastic," their chief science officer said, his expression belying the claim. "I am *fully* committed to making the best of this situation."

The way most of them were acting, Gervais would have thought they'd just been marooned on an uninhabited planet. Bauman claimed to be enthusiastic but looked aggressive instead of committed. Evans was giving off an air of resentment that probably stemmed from the impression that her specialty would be deemed unnecessary.

They had all set out from Earth with the aim of finding a place for a colony. They had plans for exploration and scientific tests to conduct and precedents to set. And then, two days ago, an unmanned mission had successfully completed all of those tasks without input from the human creators. Their mission had been hailed as pioneering and they were now due to arrive as an interstellar Habit for Humanity crew. Gervais couldn't fault them for a little disappointment.

"The enthusiasm is for giving ourselves new purpose," he reminded them. "You all took initiative when you signed up to be part of the command crew, so I'd like to hear that same drive put to work now that we need a new dream to achieve."

"And that's where the beauty of modern technology comes in?" Evans guessed, glancing back at Dujardin with a slight grin on her face.

"Exactly."

"Care to elaborate?" Gervais prompted.

The commander should have known that Dujardin would elaborate rather elaborately. It had only been a few hours since the call for a meeting had been made, so he couldn't make anything in 3-D, but he had a presentation prepared and that inspired an eye roll from everyone but the lecturer.

"We aren't going to be the first to find a place to call home, but we can be the first to make a home on a distant world. I'm not talking about simply duplicating the bot build," he said before Bauman could object. "I'm saying that we use their data to set up what should have been the goal of the *next* mission: actual colonization. We'll set the benchmarks for supplies and create the standards for a quality of life beyond our own planet. After all, there are people already on waiting lists for migration and EC would be grateful to us for thinking so far ahead."

"There are only twelve of us, so I hope you're not planning on building a city and driving out indigenous peoples," Evans interjected.

There was a sudden spark of inspiration in his eyes. "No, but there are some other things we can do with our time and you're on the right track. Colonies are established when we take over an area, plant crops, and establish housing."

That sounded much more within their reach and no one objected to this. Gervais waved a hand to invite him to go on.

"We have the equipment to test for places where crops can be grown and we have the supplies to take that a few steps further."

"Supplies?" Bekah Bauman interrupted. "We have enough seeds for an experimental crop on a mission that will last a month."

"And the food," Dujardin continued.

"The food we need to consume until we get there," Gervais said so Bauman could discern an ally in her thought process. "There are ways to conserve that, but you're proposing something much more complicated than a mission base."

The maddening glint in Dujardin's eyes flared once again, but he managed to not mention modern technology in his next sentence. "There are other ways of conserving resources. There was a risk that one of us would need to be put into stasis until we could get proper medical care."

"You want to put twelve people into Cryosleep so we can plant space wheat when we set foot on a brave new world?" Gervais concluded.

"Not necessarily wheat, but you're getting the idea."

Gervais immediately regretted having grown up with a love for Arthur C. Clarke books. There was no HAL 9000 as far as he knew, but there were risks with putting their lives in the hands of an automated process. Expedition control could direct the necessary ship's functions, but there was a danger.

To his surprise, Evans adopted a thoughtful expression. "That would certainly demand a lot fewer calories per crewman on the way there," she said.

"The food can be preserved that long," Bauman said. "I'd want more input from the people back home before deciding anything, but I know that they took precautions in case we were unable to clean out the pantry."

That was the polite way of saying that a team had studied ways to ensure that food could remain intact and edible if the crew died or abandoned ship and it was left to be found by whoever came along next.

"And speaking of input," Gervais said, "before any of us agree that this is a beauty of modern technology, I'd like to hear from the doctor who would be our official cryonicist on board."

"He should be along shortly," Dujardin responded. "He was just wrapping up an evaluation –"

"I'd like to hear from him in a private chat." Gervais sighed. "This is a good start, but let's not plan the party just yet."

He didn't want to say that he secretly hoped this would be much more fun than soil samples and geographic surveys.

Dr. Westover was a hard sell – he was personally invested in doing no harm to himself or the eleven others – but he was a pushover compared to the Administration. That required proposals, evaluations, inventories, and a personal interview with each of the crew members.

No one made their vote public. It was easy to tell who was the most interested in this experiment, but when the resulting tally said that it had passed 9-3, no one openly admitted to opposing the plan.

They were here to take orders and, given no escape routes, they could not make other plans for the months to come. Gervais offered to discuss any concerns privately, but when no one came forward, he figured that they would resolve any issues when taking stock upon waking.

The greatest delay was a sort of supplemental medical school for Westover. While the others corresponded with engineers to make the best use of their building materials, and the science division focused heavily on things like botany and theoretical biology, Westover developed his skills in vitrification and learned about the latest developments in cryogenic pathology.

Reidman, the software engineer, spent a great deal of time automating processes to send emergency alerts to Expedition Control and developing remote overrides should it be necessary for EC to call off their long nap.

And through it all, Dujardin kept doggedly touting "the beauty of modern technology."

The last commentary from EC was slightly nervous-sounding, but the message sounded as though they were on the Lieutenant's side: "Good luck, *Persephone*. Here's hoping the modern technology is as beautiful as your first officer says it is."

Gervais must have had hundreds of dreams, but the one about hiking the Appalachian Trail was interrupted by a persistent beeping. From the pace of it, he guessed it was a heart monitor. He processed the sound of respiration before realizing he was breathing fairly deeply. And to his relief, he didn't seem to have fallen asleep in an awkward position that would leave him with a five-month crick in his neck.

When Gervais got around to opening his eyes, it was to find that Westover was making notes on the tablet usually reserved for medical records as if the commander had just come out of a sleep study.

"G'morning, Westie," he mumbled. "I hope you slept well."

After a few questions of the "Rate your pain on a scale from 1-10" variety, the doctor handed him a blanket to wrap around his shoulders and moved on to the next crew berth.

Gervais was a creature of habit, so naturally he skipped all other stages of curiosity in favor of checking on the ship's systems. There were thousands of notifications on the computer – he'd let Dujardin handle those personally – but the only ones flagged were actual messages from EC staff.

Kaki Olsen

His gaze fell on the calendar and found it to be December 24 by EC standard.

"Any interesting reading?" Dujardin asked.

Rather than send every notification alert to him immediately, Gervais tapped the screen to highlight the relevant part of the communique. "They've been keeping an eye on our destination and think they've got a good landing strip for us."

"Excellent." There was a yawn in his subordinate's voice, but he sounded happy in a semi-conscious kind of way. "ETA?"

"Tomorrow," he said. "When you're more awake, you'll probably consider it a Christmas miracle."

"I like the sound of that," Dujardin said predictably. "Don't you?"

Gervais had no problem with being able to make a landing on any specific date, but he gave the first officer a slanting glower. "Bah!"

"Humbug," Dujardin added. "Think there's anything to eat around here?"

Gervais welcomed each of the crew over the next few hours, redistributing messages or answering routine questions about the prep for landing. Westover made sure he ate and paused for a routine physical.

He didn't give any more thought to the date until the next day, when Bensalem set them down on a planet that they'd been referring to as Class I-221 on all official correspondence. After assessing the air quality and doing some preliminary meteorological scans for the valley in which they'd landed, they suited up as a precaution and disembarked with a sense of excitement that not even Bauman could restrain.

"The Commander won't call the timing of this a holiday miracle," Dujardin proclaimed for posterity and the official EFSA transmission, "but as the date is auspicious, I've taken the liberty of designating the settlement for official purposes."

No one, not even the occasional Scrooge among them, objected to the establishment of Camp Ebenezer.

We Three Little Green Kings

Scott Ashby

wyrdd strode onto the bridge of his starship and seated himself in the center seat, where he could see his senior crew at their workstations. He listened patiently as each of his department heads gave their morning report. All was well in his ship; all was well in his world.

"Have we yet determined on which of the planets He is to be born?" he asked.

All sounds on the bridge ceased.

"We have had a team going through all the holy texts, sir," said his science officer, Ya'ax, "and we've determined it's a planet named Grime."

"I see, Ya'ax. And why are we not yet on course to Grime?"

"Well, sir, that would be because the astronomers are now attempting to ascertain the location of the planet in question. It's not listed on any chart we have."

There was a long pause.

"Is it a matter of simply not having the relevant chart?"

Gwyrdd directed the question to the ship's navigator, Kakariki.

Kakariki sat a little straighter in her chair, even while she continued to bend over her controls. Gwyrdd wondered how she could manage that.

"No, sir," Kakariki said, "It's a matter of Grime not being on any charts. The planet has not yet been discovered."

Gwyrdd's heart sank. How could they bring the gifts to the Creator if they couldn't find the right planet?

"Do we have any clues that might help?"

Kakariki shrugged. "There's a team in the philosophy department studying all the depictions of Grime in the folklore. In the meantime, we're heading for the universe center, so we'll be as close as possible to all coordinates when they've figured it out."

"Good plan. How do they think descriptions of folklore will help?"

"The working theory," Ya'ax said, "is that descriptions of the landscape, including the colors of sky, sun, weather, and vegetation, will give us an idea of the sort of planet we're looking for. Physical classifications of the inhabitants and creatures will help, telling us what sort of system would produce those types. Assessments of current technology will narrow down the planets, as well. Once we have a good idea of the planet and its environs, we'll have to search among the charted but not yet investigated planets in the outer fringes of known space to find a matching planet. Even then, it's a slim chance we'll locate the right one in time."

"Which is why we're not the only ship on this mission," grumbled Gwyrdd, more to himself than to his crew. They wisely did not answer his rhetorical remark.

Three days later, the search team from the philosophy department wrote a report with the defining criteria. A week later, the astronomy department produced three sets of coordinates that fit. Captain Gwyrdd looked at the star charts with the three sets of coordinates marked and chose the middle system.

As a youth, he'd been fond of the finger-length frosted cream-filled cakes that came three to a package. Probably because it was more protected from drying out by its mates, he'd always eaten the middle one last, feeling that it tasted best. He'd had a fondness and mostly unconscious preference for middle things since then.

He gave the order, Kakariki plotted the course, and the helmsman, Hijau, set their disc-shaped ship into motion. Gwyrdd retired to his cabin to amuse himself for the length of the journey. He'd only be needed to listen to morning reports and arbitrate disagreements between departments for the next year as they traveled to Grime. In the meantime, he was enjoying the four-dimensional virtual jigsaw puzzle he was working on.

Gwyrdd made certain he was on the bridge when they arrived and began orbiting Grime. While they were on their way, the folklorists had determined the general area where they needed to be, and had figured out the appropriate costumes, then programmed holo-emitters so they would look like the indigenous people. As they'd come within sensor range of Grime, the landing party had lost many hours of sleep in learning the local language, and spent many daytime hours learning the holy folklore and what, exactly, they should say, and to whom. The engineering team had also prepared three skimmers to look and move like local transport beasts.

Gwyrdd, Kakariki, and Ya'ax donned their holo-emitters and costumes, stood near the prepared skimmers, and then the engineers used their particle transmitters to transfer them to the surface.

They had to skim very slowly toward the city so they looked like they were actually riding on the transport beasts. When they got to the large city, well, large by local standards, they got an audience with the king by pretending to be kings themselves. When they finally got in to see him, they asked him, in accordance with the prophecies, "Where is he that is born King of the Jews? for we have seen his star in the east and are come to worship him."

Predictably, there was a bit of kerfuffle while the locals did their own research and provided them with better directions, but eventually they were able to deliver the gifts and use their disguised skimmers to get far enough out into the desert to transmit back to their ship without their disappearance being noticed.

Gwyrdd did leave one scary moment out of their report. There had been a full minute while they'd been talking to the local king, that his holo-emitter had flickered back and forth between local and natural appearances. He just hoped that the locals wouldn't eventually end up with a belief that all aliens were little green men like him.

Rudolph, the Red-Bulbed Recon Drone

Kaki Olsen

Note: While this is a clear reference to a certain reindeer, elements of this story were inspired by a story my Grandma Nelson told me of a Christmas when they thought no Christmas would arrive and were proved wrong. Ellie and Barker are named for Eunice Elizabeth and Leo Barker Nelson, my favorite role models.

"We can't wait that long."

Both sides at least agreed on that. They had disputed the need for the shipment, the contents, and the delivery date, but delays were no longer an option.

"If we don't leave in the next two hours, we won't be able to get through that storm for a couple of days," Quartermaster Barker said.

He had been impatient with the stalling since the dire needs of the outpost were transmitted, but that had been thirty-six hours ago and now he was ready to simply abscond with everything he could pack into a craft and let the procrastinators fire him when he got back. The entire argument hinged on whether what was left behind would be enough for the people who might need assistance before the next delivery.

"We can't wait that long on the basis of weather," Barker clarified, "and Camp Price might be a thing of the past if we hold off on bringing them aid."

He could show examples of precedent in detail from near and distant history and had a presentation file on hand in case it came to that, but he hated the person he became when forced to use pie charts.

He was about to use his most effective weapon – a direct and challenging stare that would dare every person in the room to oppose the right course of action – when someone else picked up the thread of conversation in a surprisingly level-headed tone.

"I will sanction the delivery as it is now planned," Councilor Martin said. "The rest of us can face a little austerity when it means life or death for a group of us."

"Thank you, Madam Councilor." There was no point in asking where this noble selflessness had been since the first request came in. He had been shown support by people of less consequence, so he was not about to challenge the leader's sudden support. "Please let it be known that, if anyone would like to contribute a little more, I will be leaving in one hour."

He escaped before Martin or any of the others could change their mind.

"So, are we on our way?" Ellie asked.

"We are cleared to go by Martin herself," Barker confirmed. "How close are we to being on our way?"

This is the moment at which she had good cause to sigh as a teacher might when asked about the reason for a child's failing grades. And their ship was *always* scoring low on some diagnostic.

"Nav is off again and I'd rather not make flying blind more than a metaphor," she answered.

"And we could use the old-fashioned way, but that wouldn't give us any data on the stormfront."

He had caught a glimpse of encroaching clouds on his way to the shuttle shed and even those had made him nervous. "How did they ever survive unknown territory in the old days?"

She cracked a sardonic smile. "I think you're forgetting the number of songs and poems having to do with 'The Wreck of the Something-or-other.' Those are just the tragedies we know the outcome of."

"Then let's not add 'The Last Voyage of the Bee' to the list," he said. "I'd rather this story be called 'The Miracle on Midinor Plains.'"

"I like it," Ellie decided after only a moment's hesitation. "But for that miracle, we still need something to guide the shuttle. We need a navigation console that can do more than blink pretty lights but I think we'll miss our window to skirt the storm."

While waiting the thirty-six hours for the go-ahead, Barker had spent a depressing amount of time looking at the data coming in from the meteorological stations. The storms were possibly going to swing to the northeast, but it was much more likely that the advisory would say to hunker down and wait for clearer skies. He just wanted to be already on his way when he was told to shelter in place and hope for the best.

The fire had sparked suddenly, spread fast, and done more damage to materiel than to population. The first flames had been glimpsed at 0247 and by 0638, the winds had generously spread them to 73% of the structures in Camp Price.

Those were the simple numbers to explain why two hundred thirteen people had been forced to call the camp hall home as of yesterday morning. It was certainly the most complex building they had out here in the shadow of the Midinor Mountains, but that meant that it had wings for offices and an auditorium. The top floor was a medical clinic with room for fifty beds. Many of those unaffected by the calamity had returned to their homes in the early hours of the day and brought as many beds as possible.

Mayor Bly had sent pictures of the destruction as well as statistics to instill a sense of urgency, but he supplemented the records with more details.

"We have beds or pallets for one hundred thirty-two and we are lucky that this takes care of most of the injured, but the clinic is overrun with patients we cannot help adequately."

The clinic was staffed by two doctors and six nurses of varying degrees of certification. They were excellent in handling concussions or broken bones, but no one before had come in with severe burns or possible internal bleeding.

The Council promised aid as soon as they heard of the tragedy, but there were long hours of waiting. When calls came in, they mentioned arrangements being made and supplies being gathered. When they managed to find a listening ear, the news was even less helpful as they were told the details of the supply run, but not the timetable.

"We have people on their way," Councilor Martin said. "They'll be in contact."

Night had already fallen on the second day and Camp Price was still pooling its resources to feed everyone and was looking for a place to store bodies of the people who did not make it through the waiting period. Bly only just managed not to say some very impolite things.

"We'll be waiting," he reminded them.

"I *think* we have a winner."

Councilor Martin did not expect to find Shuttle BP-2187-B-6 still in the shed, but the calls to their comm had gone unanswered and she had gone to investigate personally.

Rather than finding an empty dock, she found herself knocked aside by the enthusiastic copilot.

"Sorry!" Ellie Jameson called over her shoulder.

Martin followed her into the shuttle. It was packed as full as was possible—and probably more than was strictly safe. Some of the goods she spied were not on the official packing list, but this late in the evening, she was here to question only one thing.

"Why are you not yet on your way?"

"Because we were worried about *losing* our way," Barker said. "But Ellie has just resolved that concern."

Without further prompting, he toggled a switch on the device in his hand and a red light began flashing. This was quickly followed by a quiet whirring sound.

"It's a drone," Martin said.

"It's a pathfinder drone," Ellie corrected. "Much more advanced."

Barker didn't mention that the statement wasn't technically true. It had better range than the usual observation drones and the sensor relays were state-of-the-art, but it was not meant for a night such as this. But they had decided to leave that information unspoken unless it was mentioned.

"We don't need it to get too far ahead," Ellie explained. "We just need to help boost its signal while it's tethered and let it do most of the navigation work."

The little drone bobbed in mid-air, flashing its bulb enthusiastically as if in eagerness to prove her right.

"Before you can speculate on what might go wrong," Barker said, emerging from the cockpit to snatch the drone up, "we have found a navigator and time is running short. So, all those not off the shuttle in the next minute will be coming along to help."

Martin found herself outside just over thirty seconds later and gazed skeptically at the cable Barker was now linking between the shuttle and the red-nosed drone. It did not look practical, but there was no time to test that theory.

"May you have clear skies," she said.

And may that thing guide your shuttle well tonight.

Almost exactly two days after the Camp Price fire, Bly was awoken by an insistent hand shaking his shoulder.

"Someone says they saw a light in the woods," Jessica informed him. "And then another person got a ping on the sensors."

He scrambled to his feet, a difficult task to accomplish at

his age and given that he was using a large packing crate as his bed. He took the tablet out of her hands. There had, in fact, been three reported sightings and two pings on the sensors. There had even been a fifteen-second burst of sound that might be a local transmission.

Not willing to take truth through second-hand accounts, Bly pulled a sweater over his pajamas and joined one of the watchmen at his tower.

"Three lights?"

"Five now." The young man looked sheepish at sharing the information, but the sensor readings implied that he wasn't hallucinating. "And..."

"Six. Seven."

The random flash of red stuttered twice, then blinked a steady hello. It had to be a signal beacon from an incoming craft. This theory was confirmed a few seconds later when a little drone appeared a few yards in front of a Council-owned shuttle.

By the time Ellie and Barker lowered the ramp and carried out the first of the pre-fab shelters, every person who was healthy enough to be roused from their beds was ready to help with the unloading. It took minutes between all of them, but like children around wrapped presents, they couldn't resist the urge to put the supplies to use. Cots unfolded in the Hall, several shelters were erected, and the most sensible person began gathering eggs for a proper breakfast.

"We can't thank you enough," Bly said sometime in the middle. "We hadn't heard anything all night, so we thought this had been called off."

"We were lucky," Ellie said, cradling the drone in both hands. "This little guy couldn't keep us out of the storm altogether, but he kept us going in the right direction all through the night."

Bly had an absurd urge to pat the thing on the head like a loyal pet, but instead tapped its still-glowing bulb fondly in recognition of what they'd all relied upon for hope.

"Luck or not, I'm sure this red-bulbed recon drone will go down in Camp Price history."

Rock-ing Around the Christmas Tree

Scott Ashby

Meadowlith nudged the controls and his ship *Asteroid Hunter* backed neatly out of the docking bay on station *Tannenbaum*. Many starships docked here for their crews to have some R&R. A lot of trading and other commerce took place here, as it did wherever humanity assembled. The *Tannenbaum* was, of course, a supply depot for all ships belonging to the Confederated Star Systems, CSS for short. However, the main purpose of the station was the same as the lighthouses on Old Earth – to protect ships from colliding with dangerous rocks. In this case, the asteroids that bounced around in the Christmas Tree Nebula.

The nebula wasn't much bigger than others, about sixty light-years long, but, unusually, it was nearly conical rather than the more usual sphere or ring shape. Also, it was a brilliant green, due to it being mostly comprised of oxygen, although hydrogen was more prominent near the tip, shining brilliantly red. In short, the nebula looked very much like a Christmas Tree, hence the name.

Rock-ing Around the Christmas Tree

The trouble, of course, was that the nebula had several groupings of asteroids rattling around inside, which hadn't been (and, most likely, never could be) completely mapped.

As the nebula was a gaseous concentration, flying a ship through a nebula couldn't cause any damage. The shields on most ships could ignore the gas and most dust particles, up to a full micron in diameter, which sounded small, but was pretty big for dust. Ships' defensive fields could pulverize more solid pieces, from the micron size on up to those about five or six inches across – about the size of a human fist. The cone-shaped "cow-catcher" shield, named for the protuberance on the front of old steam locomotives, performed much the same job of deflecting obstacles directly in the vehicle's path. It could deal with anything up to the size of a domicile, but it was expensive in terms of energy, and only turned on in areas where large rocks were expected.

The better choice for passenger and cargo ships was to avoid the area entirely, and most did, except for tourists who liked flying through nebulae. However, for the best safety of both sightseers and the scientists studying the nebula, the small scout ships went out daily on both near and far mapping expeditions, because if you knew where the rocks were, then you also knew where your ship shouldn't go.

Meadowlith programmed in the course that would take him to the edge of the explored portion of the nebula, where his mission would begin in earnest. He'd be going to the southern part of the Cepheus C area of the nebula, where new stars were being born. His job on this trip was to get the scanning equipment close enough to the six-light-year long section of the nebula to catalog and classify the newest stars.

Once fully on course, he locked the controls down out of

habit, despite the fact that he knew he was the only living thing on the *Asteroid Hunter*. Safe habits were often the one thing that kept pilots alive when things went wrong. He unstrapped and went aft to the crew quarters, where he fixed himself a meal and prepared for bed. It would take a full dozen days to reach his assigned area, so he had plenty of time to himself.

The alarm klaxon rang. Meadowlith was instantly awake, and just as fast, he knew what the problem was. The whistling of air told him everything he didn't want to know. He grabbed the tabletop, unlatched it, and laid it flat on the floor. The vacuum of space did the rest; the remaining air pressure in the crew quarters pressed the table securely against the small hull breach, making a temporary patch. He'd have to install a permanent patch in the floor, and then suit up and go EVA to weld another permanent patch over the other end of the hole in the ship's skin. He'd also have to make patches in the decks and ceilings of the other affected compartments between the crew quarters and the outer hull.

That wasn't the worst problem he had at the moment.

The blast doors – the hatch into the room and, he knew, the hatches in the ventilation system and at both ends of this section of the ship – had done their job, sealing the crew quarters off from the rest of the ship. Although the leak was no longer leaking, at least in this compartment, the crew quarters had a lower air pressure than the rest of the ship, and no further atmosphere would be allowed into the area until the computers had been reset…from the cockpit.

Meadowlith immediately resolved to have secondary

controls installed in the crew quarters, where he spent much of his time, but that wasn't going to help him now.

He dug out the small toolkit he kept in here for the nearly-continual adjustments the catering unit demanded, and removed the faceplate over the door controls, hoping to find a way to encourage them to open. There were too many wires, thick, thin, and in a variety of colors, running off to too many different parts of the ship, and none of them were labeled. He wasn't about to try short-circuiting the door without more information – what if he killed the life support system – or the lights – first?

He screwed the access panel back into its proper position.

He powered up the catering computer, and started looking at menus, hoping he could somehow interface with the main computer, and get it to release more atmosphere into the crew quarters, or at least open the doors so he could get back to the cockpit and start fixing things.

Meadowlith looked at the chronometer and sighed. He was ten days and fifteen hours out from base. It was well over a day until the ship would reach its pre-programmed coordinates, and if he didn't give any further instructions, the ship would simply remain stationary. Even if he could get a distress call off, it would take eleven days until he could be rescued. While he could eat, evacuate, and sleep, he didn't have eleven days of oxygen in the crew quarters. And the guys back at the base would never let him live this one down. Trapped in his own crew quarters, sheesh!

He continued to dig through the app menus, looking for anything that might be of help. He couldn't find anything that looked at all helpful, although there were many apps he couldn't identify, and he was too much of a coward to run a program when he didn't know what it did.

Maybe 'coward' wasn't the right word. Maybe he should say he was too prudent a pilot to run a program when he didn't know what would happen. Yeah, prudent sounded a lot better than cowardly.

Meadowlith went to bed that night, but with his worries about running out of oxygen, he had a lot of trouble falling asleep. In the middle of the night, three facts that blended together into a single idea brought him bolt upright and wide awake.

The *Asteroid Hunter*'s black boxes were buried in the panels behind the catering equipment. There were other ships out on mapping expeditions that were closer to him than the base was. And finally, if he could cause enough trauma to one of the black boxes, it would go off automatically, and any – and every – nearby ship would come investigating.

Leftovers from planetary-based aviation, the so-called black boxes had several components. One was the flight data recorder that collected all information about a flight from course and engine settings to everything said in the cockpit. One part was the emergency locator transmitter, that sent out a signal so the wreckage could be more easily found. In the old days, a hard landing was enough to set one off, but in today's era of space travel, it took the acceleration of a full crash to make one start transmitting the emergency signal – or possibly throwing the box to the floor several times would be enough.

Meadowlith brought up the lights, got out the toolbox, and started digging into the panel. This had better work, or…well, no, he would run out of oxygen before he could starve to death. In short order, he had the catering equipment half-disassembled and laying on one of the crew bunks, carefully strapped down against sudden acceleration or deceleration. Old habits died hard.

He found the pair of bright orange boxes and removed them from their cubby in the wall. They were clearly marked "Flight Data Recorder" and "ELT." He violently ripped the wires from the ELT, then hurled the box as hard as he could at the wall on the other side of the room. He knew the box had a battery back-up that would activate when the power supply from the ship was cut and hoped that cutting the power supply would be enough in itself to activate the box's transmitter.

He walked across the room, picked up the box, and hurled it against the opposing wall, repeating this action several times before he realized that the distance to the wall was actually decreasing the amount of shock he was inflicting on the box, as well as making him use more oxygen. He commenced hurling the box against the floor instead.

Suddenly a squealing noise came through the speakers, along with a recorded voice from the ship's AI telling him an ELT signal had been activated nearby, and advising the crew to investigate it. He sighed with relief. He'd successfully sent a message for help.

Unfortunately, he couldn't shut off the AI, so he'd be listening to his own distress beacon until help came, whenever that was.

He reassembled the catering equipment and put it back into its cabinet, so at least he would have both food and water until help came. He searched all the crew lockers and found a dozen rebreathers – masks that salvaged oxygen from what you breathed out and let you rebreathe the same air until all the oxygen was gone. Each was good for about five hours, so that would give him about two and a half more days of breathing, once he'd used as much of the oxygen in the room as he could.

He didn't have to wait that long. It was only fifteen hours after he'd successfully set off the ELT that he heard the first scratching noises on the hull, the sounds and vibrations of the airlock being cycled, the footsteps of pressure-suited people stomping through the *Asteroid Hunter*, and, best of all, the sound of more air entering the room through the ventilation system.

Once his rescuers released the blast doors, he was able to help them make repairs to the hull and lift the table from its place on the floor.

They found the walnut-sized meteorite embedded in the crew quarters' ceiling, and Meadowlith pocketed it as a souvenir.

They were able to deactivate the ELT, and shut off the horrible whining in the speakers, as well as the AI's complaint that the beacon needed to be followed immediately.

The pilots who'd rescued him went back to their work, and Meadowlith turned his poor *Asteroid Hunter* back to base, where he'd be able to get better repairs, and also have a secondary control computer installed in the crew quarters.

I Wonder as I Wander Out Among the Stars

Kaki Olsen

Note: I have spent a total of forty-three months as a missionary in my life and often think of ways in which missionary work would work in fictional settings. This story is in memory of Sister Peggy Lee, a friend and dedicated missionary lost during the COVID-19 pandemic.

"This is it?"

There were dozens of books on every aspect of missionary work, all written from a position of experience and good intentions. Sister Haydn had eschewed them all in favor of official materials. There were lessons to be learned from scriptural sources and manuals, teachers who would impart everything she needed to know about taking the gospel to every person she came across during her service as an official representative.

No one had mentioned that doing things "by the book" would leave her to rely on something that was thinner than her personal journal.

I Wonder as I Wander Out Among the Stars

"This is uncharted territory," President Lee said, "almost literally."

It was true that she was going to be companions with a missionary native to a world she'd never heard of before today. They would both speak English, even if they might have different slang for things, but would have very little shared experience otherwise.

"Think of it this way," he prompted. "The first Christian missionaries left the civilizations they knew and the cultures that were familiar to them and still had great success because they were led by the spirit and common truths. Think of yourself as a Peter or Paul."

Her first thought was of Peter and the other apostles on the day of Pentecost, when Parthians and Cretes and Arabians – those from Pamphylia – were able to understand the gospel in their own tongues. She suspected that President Lee would bring up such gifts of the spirit if she expressed any doubts about making herself understood.

"I'm trying to," Sister Haydn admitted, "but we don't know who we'll find out there and we don't know what they'll need."

His answering smile was sympathetic but suggested that he had heard this sort of thing before. "You'll find children of God," he said, "and they'll need the good word of God, just like everyone else. I think you can't go wrong with those things in mind."

The Missionary Training Vessel was unable to drop Sister Haydn off at the nearest station, but she managed to reach her rendezvous in only three legs. It took two weeks and three days in total and she worried about keeping her companion waiting for most of that time.

"Welcome to Point Divergence," her last host greeted her as she set her suitcases down. "Long trip?"

"It's just nice to be on ground instead of a deck again," Sister Haydn answered.

Point Divergence had been established long enough that the receptionist could have no idea what she meant. There were people on this base who had been *born* here and she had to restrain herself from making that her first question.

"I'm supposed to meet Sister Ford here," she said while showing her proselyting license and passport. "Do you know where she can be found?"

A minute of typing later, the receptionist shook her head. "It looks like she has an even longer trip to make," she commented. "We can make you comfortable here until she arrives, of course."

Sister Haydn wasn't exactly comfortable being unaccompanied, but here in atmosphere, they had room to build and the guest quarters at PD were larger than anything she'd had on the trip from the MTV to the rendezvous. She unpacked the essentials, turned up the alerts on her phone, and went to bed as soon as she'd said her nightly prayers.

There were no messages about Sister Ford the next morning, but she followed the map that was attached to her wake-up call and got breakfast. She ate the first scrambled eggs she'd had in months while talking to a couple who were about to board a ship bound for their ancestral homeworld of Earth.

Her family had left two generations ago from Europe and they were descended from Japanese explorers, but that was common enough ground to make the conversation enjoyable.

On Day 2, she bid them farewell and lingered at the arrivals port, but there was still no sign of Sister Ford. She took her study materials to the hotel garden, and no one interrupted her.

On Day 3, she finally awoke to a message saying that Sister Ford would meet her for breakfast. It took everything she had to dress first and head to the dining room after, but she arrived in a skirt and blouse and immediately looked for the person who would have a similar nametag to hers.

Since there were only ten people in the room, it wasn't hard to spot the other missionary. She even had the same display on her nametag that cycled through languages and pictographic systems and that small detail was a strange comfort.

"You must be Sister Haydn," the older woman greeted her. "I hope I didn't keep you waiting long."

Her senior companion didn't ask too many questions while they ate, but that changed as soon as Sister Ford helped her move her things into the room they'd be sharing until their departure.

"Are you nervous?"

The answer was 'yes,' but she didn't want to make a bad impression, so she opted for an answer to a different question. "I feel unprepared."

The smile on Sister Ford's face was not unlike President Lee's and she now recognized it as shorthand for "We've all felt that way."

"If ye are prepared, ye shall not fear," Sister Ford quoted. "I'm nervous, too."

Sister Haydn had to wonder if she'd been given the same ten-page pamphlet or if she had more materials in her suitcase. "Then how do we prepare? There's no guide for this."

"Which is why we prepare together," her companion said confidently. "Our first assignment is on a ship bound for a planet that has signs of life. If that turns out to be inaccurate, we can still help the scientists who will be doing surveys and preach the gospel with words if necessary."

That was exactly what they did two days later. Three weeks were spent in service while the zoologist and botanist and geologist began the encyclopedia entries for the planet. Two of the crew were interested in spiritual matters, but by the time they returned to PD, they had a new assignment.

The second excursion was bringing supplies to a colony who had experienced severe earthquakes and needed extra supplies. This was the first time the Sisters were able to attend church since being sent unto every nation, but they spent their days in service and their evenings in teaching.

They had just touched down at PD when a new itinerary came in from Missionary Travel, to leave the same day.

"Someone's made first contact," Sister Ford explained. "They're still working on communication, but these people have never met humans before and that's where we come in."

The trip was to take almost as long as the journey to Point Divergence, but they had a destination and a people to reach out to.

"President Lee told me that when we found people, they would be just like us," Sister Haydn recalled. "Children of God who needed the gospel."

Sister Ford was meant to be the more experienced teacher, but they were on equal footing here and she looked thoughtful at the description. "I was sent here by President Sciaparelli, who had a slightly different name for them. 'Other sheep.'"

They had spent a lot of companionship study on what that

meant over the few months since their rendezvous and had come up with some basic truths that had to be shared before talking about anything else:

These were children of God.

These were children of the same God as the one who sent His Son to a small city called Bethlehem on a distant planet called Earth.

They needed to know that the Christ child had been born for them, no matter if they had never heard of a place called Galilee.

There were other doctrines to teach, but as they couldn't yet tell how to communicate all of that to their brothers and sisters, they set out for first contact with the truth President Sciaparelli had quoted.

"Other sheep I have, which are not of this fold. Them also must I bring."

O Little Moon of Death, Mayhem

Scott Ashby

leuad wished she could shift her useless body and looked out the window again. It was said by her people that if someone was ill, they should expose all their skin to the first beams of the rising full moon on the last night of the year, and they would be healed. There were only a few problems with that idea.

The first was that it was only full on the last night of the year, once every nineteen years. The second problem was that her parents didn't follow the old ways, but had embraced the new religion. They believed public nudity was an evil thing, or if not precisely evil, immoral, and would not help her. The third was that she couldn't get out into the moonlight, with or without clothing, by herself.

She'd been born on a full moon night. Tomorrow, she would be nineteen, an old maid. Nobody wanted to court a woman who couldn't move out of her bed on her own, much less marry one. And tomorrow, also, was the first time the moon would be full on the last night of the year since the day she'd been born.

O Little Moon of Death, Mayhem

She'd been born hung, wrapped in the mother's rope, and not breathing. A few days later, her parents noticed that although she could cry and eat, she never moved. The healer had told them her inability to move was because of being wrapped in the mother's rope.

The strange thing about her affliction was that, although she could not move any part of her body, she had sensation. She could feel soft and hard, hot and cold, and so forth, while others who had suffered a broken neck and were paralyzed could not. The witch doctor said she was a lost soul and instructed her parents to leave her in the jungle as an offering to Karissa, the moon goddess.

Instead, they had named her Lleuad, after the small moon that circled their planet, and nursed her constantly, feeding and cleaning her, and seeing that she got an education.

The moon gleamed different colors in different parts of her cycle, and could appear as every color between silver and red. When she was red, she supposedly caused madness and death.

Tomorrow, the moon would be full on the last day of the year; additionally, the witch doctor had calculated that, near midnight, the sky wolves would not only turn the dusky red moon its deepest shade, but that they would actually eat the moon and then throw it back. A special moon, indeed.

Lleuad had had words with her brother Anghrian and arranged with their parents that she would spend this year-beginning with him in the great city. Although her brother had also adopted the new religion, he respected Lleuad's beliefs in clinging to the old ways. He would help her, tomorrow night, to expose her skin to the reddish moon of death and mayhem. He'd be coming for her this afternoon.

126

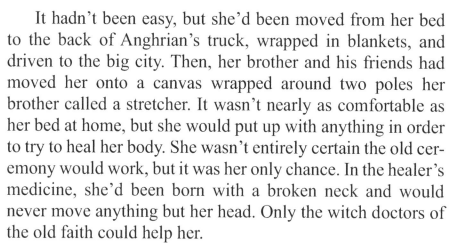

It hadn't been easy, but she'd been moved from her bed to the back of Anghrian's truck, wrapped in blankets, and driven to the big city. Then, her brother and his friends had moved her onto a canvas wrapped around two poles her brother called a stretcher. It wasn't nearly as comfortable as her bed at home, but she would put up with anything in order to try to heal her body. She wasn't entirely certain the old ceremony would work, but it was her only chance. In the healer's medicine, she'd been born with a broken neck and would never move anything but her head. Only the witch doctors of the old faith could help her.

As it grew time for sunset and moonrise on the last day of the year, Anghrian's friend came and helped move her to the roof of the building where he lived. The two men put up privacy curtains so that no one would be able to see her naked body, a concession to the new religion and teachings of her parents, so they would not be offended if they ever found out.

The friend left, and her brother lovingly removed her clothing, exposing Lleuad's skin. The breeze racing across the rooftop was cold, and Lleuad's skin stood up in chicken-zits. The tips of her fingers turned numb, and Anghrian said they were blue.

Another of Anghrian's friends arrived, a witch doctor of the old religion, and he performed a ceremony, ritually cleansing her. They waited until it was time for the moonrise, and the witch doctor opened the privacy curtain to allow the moon's first rays entry. Anghrian checked and told her that there was no one else out on the roof to see her, so that she could tell her parents that no one had seen her without clothing except for Anghrian and the doctor she had consulted.

The sun blazed its last, heatless light and slipped below the edge of the world as the moon rose into visibility, bathing Lleuad's skin in its angry red light.

After gaining Lleuad's consent to the entire ceremony, the witch doctor sent Anghrian away, then performed the healing ceremony, which involved flicking Lleuad's skin with various feathers, dripping oils and sacred water on various parts of her body, vigorously rubbing the oils into her skin – often in places no man outside her family had ever seen, much less touched before, and drawing signs against evil in particular paints made with certain oils and pigments. A small tattoo was made on her shoulder, a sun and moon design, intended to bind the magic into her body so the healing would be as permanent as the design. There was a lot of chanting.

Once Lleuad looked at the sky and realized the moon was only a small sliver of dark red, nearly invisible against the black sky and stars. The witch doctor continued to work over her all but lifeless body, rubbing in more oils, coloring with paints, and always softly chanting, until the moon dropped below the horizon and the sun rose once again, on the first day of the year.

He told her the ritual was done, and that she would heal, but it would take time, and work, and nothing would happen at all until she became a mother. He also told her the healing ceremony must be renewed each time there was a full moon on the last day of the year. He left her, then, lying on the roof-top, naked and alone.

Lleuad wept. She knew she would never be a mother. A man married a woman to bear his children, and to care for them, and him, and his household. Although she supposed she was technically able to have children, what man would marry a bed-bound, useless lump such as herself?

Anghrian returned, covered her with a sheet, and fetched his friend to help carry her down the stairs to his apartment. The friend waited in the outer room while Anghrian bathed and dressed her. The friend helped carry her useless body out to the back of Anghrian's truck, and Anghrian drove her home. At least she could tell her parents that the fireworks at midnight, as seen from Anghrian's roof, far surpassed those of their village, her purported reason for spending the holiday with her brother.

There had been a huge uproar in March when she was found to be with child. Lleuad knew this child was a result of the healing ceremony. The local witch doctor proclaimed that since Lleuad couldn't go out, the devil had come to her in the night, and that she should drink potions of his own making to shake the child loose from her womb.

She refused.

Her parents had the priest of the new religion come in to exorcize and bless her, but she refused to see him, too. Most of her village regarded the growing child as a miraculous birth, and either feared or honored her. The healers watched over her, and as the autumn leaves turned as deep red as the moon had turned that night, she delivered the son that had grown in her womb.

Her mother complained at having to deal with two who were equally helpless. The nurse held the child to Lleuad's breast to drink, and Lleuad's arms suddenly curled around the babe, holding him safely against her.

The healing came swiftly after that, as she was able to do each thing her son needed, caring for him herself, and slowly gaining the use of her own body.

When her son was two, one of the young men of the village who was about her age came courting and, after a proper time, they married.

That was when she became sure that her son had been planted in her by the witch doctor in the city, and she wondered if that was truly part of the healing ceremony, or his own addition. She didn't care. She had a son, and the use of her body, and now a husband. She would have paid that price twice over if she were asked again. She would certainly go into the city and see him again in sixteen years, when it was time for the ceremony to be renewed.

Joy to the Other Otherworld

Kaki Olsen

here was a special challenge whenever community efforts needed to be coordinated across a solar system. This was brought to mind every time the respective planetary governments held conferences, but it was also true of system-wide educational initiatives. Every settlement had a zone coordinated to GMT on Earth for reference, but that meant that many people experienced things in the morning while others had to rouse themselves in the middle of the night or wait for a rebroadcast.

This was a special occasion, of course, and there was no question of excluding someone because it would mean staying up past their bedtime.

Astronauts had been exploring habitable planets and moons for centuries, but it was a fairly new thing to bring people who were still learning their letters along for the ride. This was the decade of diaspora and with so many people having their first Christmas at their new home, it was time to make it the most wonderful time of the year in as many orbits as possible.

Joy to the Other Otherworld

Some pundits called it silly and sentimental. Others commented on the estimated costs to coordinate everything and published pieces on how they could better use the funds pooled together to give everyone a happy holiday. These were immediately countered by examples of other holidays being celebrated as near as Artemis Base and as far as the station known as Outpost Ganymede.

"There are technological obstacles to broadcasting simultaneously, so no matter how carefully you plan it, this will be a disappointment for *someone*," one commentator claimed.

That was true. They couldn't be sure that there wouldn't be interference. There were delays in getting signals across that much space. It would take time for the video and audio to be cleaned up.

The adults found any number of reasons to complain, but this had been the idea of the children and they couldn't resist making their best effort.

The question had been asked, "What would it be like if Mary and Joseph came to somewhere other than Bethlehem?" They could not have a simulcast of life on every world, but they welcomed presentations of all kinds.

The most enthusiastic response was from the first colony to try domesticating animals. There weren't exactly shepherds watching over their flocks by night, but there was a place in Zone 23 nicknamed The Pasture and every child enrolled in the school spent some of their week tending to the furry, deer-sized animals that they called marfs for the noises they made. No one minded that the marfs didn't like to stay still for very long because most of the animals were transported and raised in a laboratory setting by adults and the marfherders got to experience the real thing.

Not to be outdone, the children nearest the Agridome on Mars showed off their stable and manger. The animals had feeding shifts and exercise periods, so baby Jesus would have had to wait his turn to be laid in a manger.

Waypoint was known to just about *everyone* either by reputation or experience, and they were proud to say that, if Mary and Joseph had come through their customs checkpoint, there would have been plenty of room for them in the housing units. They even had a man who looked like Santa Claus in charge of stores, so there was no question that it wouldn't have been a problem *there*.

There weren't any settlements on Satellite 1225, but there were computers so advanced that they were almost like people themselves. They were in charge of census data and one of the human analysts who reaped the data took Luke, Chapter 2, Verses 1-5 as his project. S-1225's contribution showed the numbers of people who had been counted in the census, but showed details of the people in their own settlements so they would know what it was like to be counted according to what house and lineage they were from.

At Outpost Ganymede, one of the finest doctors beyond earth showed the children how to swaddle a baby using the clothes she had manufactured herself. She didn't go so far as to explain how babies were delivered, for which everyone was thankful.

With the communications challenges in mind, the oldest participants were the people who designed interplanetary communications arrays. They were the ones to show how it might have been possible for an angel of the Lord to send a message to everyone who needed to know that "unto you is born this day in the City of David, a Savior who is Christ the

Lord." The relay satellites were dubbed the multitude of the heavenly host for the time being.

Even with that demonstration, the most impressive contribution was courtesy of an astrophysicist parent who could use one of the most powerful telescopes known to man to look for a star in the east. They managed to relay the data widely enough that children could be gathered to witness the star for themselves and, like the wise men from the east, see the star of the newborn savior.

On Earth, one family was able to make the 90-mile journey from Nazareth to Bethlehem. This was farther from home than many of the children had ever been and even though there were modern buildings and craft on the road instead of people traveling by donkey between inns, it was a wonderful sight to see.

There was no practical way to reach everyone at once, but the broadcast came from Earth on the stroke of midnight on Christmas Day. It was up to the children if they wanted to watch in their homes or if they should gather in a more public place. In Zone 23, the marfherders watched the broadcast while abiding in their own fields.

No matter the challenges and doubts, there was joy to many worlds and everyone was invited to let their settlement receive their King.

Red Shirts Roasting on an Open Fire

Scott Ashby

A Cavaliers Story

It was graduation time again, and most of the fleet was at Terradia, waiting to pick up their graduates or transport graduates going elsewhere to their posts.

Many Cavaliers had leave time coming, and Jenna was one of them. She was going backpacking with Lissanne, Skylar, and Kiernan. She shoved the last of her gear into her jump bag, checked that the civilian clothing she was wearing was all in place – she felt naked without her laser, but it wasn't allowed with civilian clothing – and the group had all agreed to leave their uniforms behind for this trip.

Everything was in order, and she hustled to the shuttle hangar to catch her scheduled ride to the planet's surface.

The ride down was uneventful, though Jenna felt a little out of place among her shipmates. She was the only person not in uniform. Relax, she told herself, it's good to get out of uniform every once in a while. And you're going off to have some fun!

As soon as the shuttle's door opened, she was out of her seat and moving. She'd left her possessions on the *Aubria*, as her assignment to that ship had been extended, so her jump bag only contained fresh clothing, including one uniform – just in case – and the survival equipment she'd be using while camping. Her gear wouldn't all fit in a small carrisack. The design of the jump bag straps meant it could be used as a backpack, though not quite as comfortably as a purpose-built pack. It would do, anyway.

As she walked to the spaceport building, Jenna absently noted that it appeared to be late afternoon, and she tapped her chrono, instructing it to switch to local planetary time.

The four friends had agreed to meet in Kiernan's quarters – as he was currently teaching, he had housing on the planet.

Jenna breezed through the Academy's spaceport building and saw Kiernan waiting for her in the lobby. She walked over and greeted him, dropping her jump bag on the floor as they hugged.

"Everyone was arriving within half a timepart of each other, so I decided to just pick you all up here. Lissanne's over there, and Skylar will be about another quarter timepart." He scooped up her jump bag, and she followed him to a grouping of chairs. Lissanne jumped up from her seat to hug Jenna, and the three of them sat down, catching up on their news as they waited.

Skylar appeared at the tail end of the next shuttle load, and Kiernan hustled them off to his quarters. "We'd need to eat before setting out to the refuge," he explained, "and by the time we get there it'll be dark anyway, so we may as well sleep here tonight and get an early start in the morning."

Scott Ashby

Teacher's quarters for single officers consisted of a bed-room, a 'fresher, and a single living area that was used as a lounge, office, kitchen, and dining room. Kiernan's three guests dropped their jump bags on the floor, out of the way against one wall of the tiny living room, while Kiernan went over to the catering unit and produced food for everyone. There weren't enough chairs, or enough table space, so they all lounged on the floor while they ate.

By the time they were finished eating, it was dark outside.

"So how early is this 'early start' you mentioned?" Skylar asked.

Kiernan's eyes twinkled with mischief, while his voice remained calm and off-hand. "0400."

"0400?" Lissanne protested in mock outrage. "0400 on vacation?"

Kiernan laughed, and they all joined him.

"The reserve is about a third of the way around the planet – a long haul by flitter. But before we get some shut-eye, you all should re-pack your jump bags. I've got some back packs that will be a lot more comfortable."

He rose and went into his bedroom, returning with one packed backpack and three empty ones, which he distributed. He also handed out the food rations they'd need to help carry. It didn't take long for the supplies and equipment to be moved into the backpacks, and for the Cavaliers to crawl into their sleeping bags and fall asleep on the floor.

0400 came with swiftness, but Kiernan, ever the consid-erate host, had risen and dressed at 0330 so he could prepare a hearty breakfast for them. With everyone helping, it only took a few minutes to clean up from the meal, heft their packs, and walk across the broad expanse of lawn to where Kiernan had parked his flitter. They stowed the packs in the rear and clambered in. Lissanne and Jenna took the slightly smaller rear seats, while the larger men sat in the front. Kiernan set the flitter in motion while Jenna and Lissanne returned to sleep, a distinct advantage to riding in the back.

It was nearing evening by the time they reached the main gate of the wildlife reserve. They grabbed their backpacks and trooped into the visitor's center, checked in, gave the caretakers their approximate route and that they planned to be there a pair of weeks.

Skylar ran the parking permit out to their flitter, moved it to the place the caretaker said they should leave it, and locked it, then returned to the group. Meanwhile, they'd sworn they'd brought their own food and were not a hunting party, which would have required them to hire a professional guide.

The hunting parties were why all guests in the reserve had to wear bright red shirts – to protect hikers and hunters alike. Rangers wore orange, while guides wore bright yellow, providing identification as well as visibility. Campers and hikers had to promise they wouldn't kill anything in the reserve, with the exception that they were allowed to take sufficient fish within a certain size bracket from lakes and streams for daily meals. They all tucked their permits into their packs, donned their provided red overshirts, and set off together into the reserve to commune with nature and deepen their friendship.

It took the next three and a half days to reach Lake Vaka-bebe and set up their base camp in a protected hollow near the shore. They took time to swim and made a wonderful dinner with trout, garlic, and campfire-heated stones.

Next morning, Jenna hooked a mini-survival kit to her belt, along with a day's supply of easily-transported food. The others had similar bags dangling from their belts as they left their camp behind, and headed out on a long hike to the reportedly-gorgeous Gloynbyw Falls, one of the highest waterfalls on Terradia.

The falls had been deliberately left isolated; there were no roads that led to them, and the only way in was on foot, without even a made and maintained path. Hikers were asked to approach from different directions, depending on the month, to avoid the creation of social trails, in order to enhance the natural beauty of the place. The number of permits to approach the falls each month was limited. No camping was permitted within three maxims of the falls.

They didn't expect to return to their base camp until long after dark, but the moon was full tonight, and all four of them were experts in navigation and survival.

The sun played hide-and-seek behind puffy white clouds as they walked. Skylar had been put in charge of navigation, and they wove in and out between the trees, spreading out a little to lessen the impact of their footsteps on the forest floor. They descended into micro-canyons several times to cross small streams on their way to Lake Vakabebe.

The terrain was rougher than they'd expected, but they reached the falls in the early afternoon and enjoyed a late luncheon that included some chocolate chip cookies Jenna had made specifically for this part of their trip.

"These are really good," Skylar said around his mouthful of cookie, "but not the same as the ones we had on Earth."

"Yes, well, Aunt Hanna's a better baker than I am. Plus, I

don't think you can get better chocolate than what grows on Earth."

"Some plants just grow better on certain planets," Lissanne said, "and not even necessarily their native homes."

They rested in the sun for a while, enjoying the unexaggerated beauty of the waterfall and the not-quite-silence of nature before starting out on their return journey. It was nearly sundown when the storm broke.

It seemed like the clouds were suddenly unzipped. The force of the rain nearly threw them to the ground; the lightning encouraged them to stay down, its shimmering bolts brighter by far than the last gleams of the westering sun.

The four of them, soaked to the skin, huddled behind and half under an old deadfall. The storm lasted an interminable quarter timepart. The sun was gone. A few stars appeared, but not enough for navigation. The strengthening breeze was sharp and cold. The Cavaliers had a quick conference without moving from their scant shelter.

"The rivers in those ravines will have risen significantly," said Skylar. "I don't fancy trying to cross them in the dark."

"Neither do I. Are we agreed that we camp here tonight?" asked Lissanne.

Jenna and Kiernan gave assenting sounds.

"Is there any food left?" Kiernan asked. They all checked their bags, and found enough for a small evening meal, if they pooled their resources. Skylar had some ration bars that would do for breakfast. Jenna shuddered with old memories of rats and ration bars, but knew she was going to have to eat at least some, if she wanted the energy to get back to their base camp tomorrow.

Skylar and Kiernan set about finding materials to build a

somewhat larger and more water-resistant shelter based around the fallen tree where they'd hidden from the storm, while Jenna and Lissanne searched for dry combustibles for a fire. They found some fallen logs that would be dry enough to burn once the sodden bark was removed. They gathered little bits of kindling hiding on the sheltered side of large bushes and the inner protected spaces in the heart of tree groupings, but there was very little in the way of mid-sized branches that would burn long enough to ignite the logs.

Finally, Jenna came up with a solution. They all shed their high visibility red over-shirts. The wicking fabric they were made of was already dry. Lissanne used a utility knife to cut them in strips. Kiernan pulled a pair of small boxes – one holding fuzzy, linty tinder and the other full of charcloth – from one pants pocket, and a steel striker and chunk of flint from another.

The flint and steel made a spark, the charcloth caught and nourished it while it was transferred to the tinder, which allowed a tiny flame that caught and grew in the kindling. Then the strips of cloth were gently fed to the fire until the smaller chips and branches were burning high enough to get the logs going. The group gave a collective sigh of relief. They would have heat and light.

By the time the fire was going, there was also shelter. Mature branches had been cut from evergreens to create the small shelter, whose open end faced the fire. Fallen needles had been scooped in as padding for the floor. They shared their food, then took turns through the night sleeping, keeping watch, and tending their small fire.

Morning dawned clear and cold. They ate one ration bar each, disassembled their shelter, made sure the fire was properly extinguished, and did all they could to return their temporary campsite to its natural state.

Skylar was right that the creeks were up, but they made the trek to their base camp safely.

The next morning, they broke camp and headed back toward the visitor's center. They couldn't legally stay in the reserve without their high visibility overshirts, so their trip was, of a necessity, cut short.

Still, it had been a fun adventure, and Jenna was grateful for the time they'd had together. She worried a little about returning to the visitor's center without the shirts they'd been issued, but she'd always be grateful for the heat from their red shirts roasting on the open fire.

Hover-sleigh Ride

Kaki Olsen

I never thought I'd miss the weather this much," Roslyn confessed.

Like everyone on board, she had to rely on everything from special lighting settings to supplements to make sure her body didn't miss anything that the great outdoors would have normally given her. Unlike thirty percent of the population, she had clear memories of the easier way of getting Vitamin D.

"You won't have to miss it much longer," Jaime said. "Haven't you read the reports?"

She turned her face away from the artificial sunlight to glower at him. "I read the reports like everyone else," she answered with a slightly grumpy tone. "Current temperature in the landing zone is consistent with temperature ranges in early autumn in the northwestern United States, with a humidity ranging between 10 and 65 percent. The air quality is considered acceptable for all groups. And we have sixteen days, twelve hours, four minutes, and...I'm not going to look up how many seconds. I miss the *weather*."

He hid a grin behind a glass of water. "So, Rosita, what you're saying is you miss the beach."

"I miss everything."

It wasn't surprising. Earth was the original home for everyone on this ship, but Jaime suspected that if they polled the population, there would be no two things that everyone missed most. For him, there was no recreating the sounds and smells of his hometown. His neighbor on the right constantly wished they had room for gardens.

Roslyn, who had grown up in New York and met him at UCLA, had talked about the storms that came in off the Atlantic, but spent a good amount of time jumping the waves at Huntington Beach. He could tell from her photographs of national parks that it wasn't as simple as finding her a coast to enjoy.

There were ships where people could pay to just pack up and leave, but the *Magellan 12* wasn't one of those. Everyone here specialized in something that they could teach or do in order to establish a society. Jaime had gotten his booking based on his ability to design cities, while his college friend was the first luthier into space and a licensed schoolteacher.

They all had a specific reason for being sixteen days out from a brave new world, but it wasn't surprising that some of them were feeling nostalgic for what they left behind.

"I'm sure you'll find something just as enjoyable as a summer night in Yellowstone," he said.

"Or skiing in Stowe," she added. "And I guarantee you that you're not the only one who will want to turn a corner of the new world into a *barrio.*"

Those were the most nostalgic things they'd allowed themselves to say in weeks and it was possibly a sign of unrealistic optimism. The planetary surveys were still cataloguing mountain ranges and valleys, what areas of land were ready for cultivation vs. what had to be tended for some time before they could put down literal roots. On the other hand, he knew that making a very adapted *elote* and playing mariachi was a far cry from the noises and smells of the San Fernando Valley.

But this was why they were both here. If they couldn't bring it with them, they could create it.

Struck by a sudden idea, he sat up straight. "Can I ask you to commit to spending time with me, no questions asked?"

It was her turn to grin. "I'll have to check my very busy schedule, but I think I can fit you in between unpacking, unpacking, and helping everyone else unpack. What date?"

"To be announced," he said. "But I promise it'll be worth it."

She raised an eyebrow, no doubt wondering which of their dreams his stroke of genius related to, but nodded. "My time is yours."

They landed a few hours ahead of schedule and found the reports to be reliable. The valley where the surveyors had set up the station had some similarities to Pennsylvania, which immediately made them feel oddly at home. As promised, Roslyn settled into her own quarters, then began dividing her time between setting up the workshops and helping to set up the classrooms in the newly-constructed school.

Jaime spent less time around the settlement since he was in high demand as a practical dreamer of dreams. His e-mails included pictures of places where he hoped to build bridges or look into plans for a dam.

The autumn proved longer than usual. As population ships began arriving, parents seemed relieved that it was still nice enough weather to let their kids run around. An actual semester would have to wait until they finished settling in, but the school became a natural gathering place for people who wanted impromptu art classes or P.E. or to just get out of their own housing for a few hours.

It was starting to feel like a community here, but it still had a way to go before any of them could consider it home.

She was so used to getting messages that it was something of a surprise when Jaime called.

"Is your time still mine?" he asked, the clarity of the signal meaning he was getting close to town.

"Within reason," Roslyn called in the direction of the speaker. "I've got choir practice in two hours."

"And after that?"

"Dinner and sleep," she said. "I can save you some dinner if you're getting close."

"Rosita, I'll take anything that can't be reconstituted from freeze-dried food." He allowed himself a chuckle. "I'll come find you at choir."

Sure enough, she saw him sneak into one of the chairs at the back during the last number. He obviously hadn't packed a razor on his last expedition, but it was such a joy to see him that she didn't mind the mountain man impersonation.

"I thought you might like that song," she said once choir was dismissed.

"I keep losing track of time, so it was something of a

surprise to hear '*O Pueblecito de Belen,'*" he answered after a quick hug.

"Well, if we're going to have a *barrio* here," Roslyn teased, "we need to start with the right music for the holidays."

"As long as it's not '*Mi Querido Santa Clos,'*" he answered.

She was willing to put up with a lot of things, but "Jolly Old St. Nicholas" was not one of them. She paused for another hug as it had been weeks since she'd gotten the chance to exchange one with him. Something about the smell of his clothing reminded her of pine forests, but that was impossible here.

"What do you have planned with my time?"

"Stop by your room for whatever dinner you had planned and bring a coat to Slip 38."

She obeyed without question and soon found him next to a hover-sleigh. "What's this?"

"You'll see."

Her only coat was made for wintry weather, but if he was planning on heading out into the wild, it was probably a good idea to not take chances. She strapped the container of food into the middle console and climbed into the passenger seat.

"We're not taking one of the closed ones," she noted.

"You won't mind soon," he said with the grin she had missed quite a lot.

It took ten minutes before they were out of reach of the settlement lights. She could still see outpost markers on various ridges, but it felt slightly eerie to be so far from officially-established civilization.

"Are you going to tell me what this is about?"

"Not yet," he answered, "but look up."

She had just obeyed when he dimmed the running lights and the newly-familiar stars became more visible. She immediately inhaled slowly and could hear his laugh.

"I thought you might like that."

"It's beautiful," she answered. "If I were in the mood to scare off local wildlife, I'd start singing about how the stars are brightly shining."

Another twenty-five minutes later, she started with surprise. "What was that?"

His laugh was even louder this time. "I didn't know you missed weather so much you forgot the name for it."

"I know what snow is," Roslyn said a bit defensively, "but the reports didn't put it on the forecast."

He turned off the lights and slowed the sleigh to a crawl. "The advantage to being best friends with Lewis or Clark is that we run across all sorts of things that aren't on the forecasts yet."

The stars were no longer brightly shining through the cloud cover that had begun to move in, but she could clearly feel a thrill of hope in her slightly-weary world.

"It's not ski season in Stowe," Jaime added, "but I hope you like it."

She could finally imagine what it would be like to find her favorite vistas here and, as she should have done all along, she imagined them with the right company.

"It's lovely weather for a hover-sleigh ride together with you," she quipped.

The snow didn't last very long before the weather decided to explore other parts of the region, but they ate their late-night dinner in satisfied silence while feeling that this place started to look familiar. They didn't have names for the black-feathered birds that swooped across their path or the skulking animals that kept pace with them closer to the ground, but they considered them as familiar as owls and possums from back home. Neither of them felt cheated as Jaime brought the engine to full power and swung the sleigh around in search of the trail back.

They rode home in companionable silence as the silent stars went by.

It's the Most Wonderful Time for the Fear

Scott Ashby

gentle vibration started at his waist, and Ambrose Wirthless grasped his pager, shut it off, and looked at it to see who he had to call.

It was the usual number, and he groaned slightly. Tonight? Seriously? They couldn't expect him to work tonight, of all nights! It was Christmas Eve, for pity's sake! He should be home with his wife, making things merry for the foster-children they'd been assigned, the poor little waifs, but no. Now, she'd have to do all the work herself, and the youngest so newly-dead that she hadn't really figured out the difference between living life and dead life yet.

Ambrose picked up the phone on his desk and dialed – why they couldn't just have cell phones here instead of the antiquated pager and land-line combinations, he didn't know.

The phone rang six times before the secretary picked it up. It always rang six times, no more, no less, and she always picked up just as the seventh ring was about to happen. The woman was nothing, if not precise. And annoying. Maybe this was his version of hell, and he hadn't gone to heaven, after all? That was something he'd been wondering for the last hundred years or so.

"Hello, Ambrose, how are you?" the secretary answered.

And how did she always know who was calling? Nobody else had any form of caller ID.

"Hi, Mary, what's up?"

"We have a visitation lined up for you for tonight. You'll be playing the Ghost of Christmas Present."

"Again? That one's so old all the corners have been rubbed off it! When and where?"

Mary chuckled. "Well, it does seem to be appropriate to use *A Christmas Carol* on Christmas Eve, somehow. You'll be going to London, in 1843, so you'll need to stop by costuming on the way."

"No problem with that; you know I do enjoy historical dress."

Mary chuckled again. "One of the reasons you got this part."

She gave him the street address, and then the name of the man he'd be visiting.

"Scrooge? Ebenezer Scrooge? You've got to be kidding me! That low-life son-of-a –"

"Language!"

"– woman," Ambrose hastily altered what he had been about to say, "But – but – hasn't he already been redeemed?"

Mary chuckled again; the sound of it was getting on Ambrose's nerves. "Not according to our records. Anyway, this isn't the guy in the story. This is the real Scrooge, the one Dickens must have based his story on. So you've got to be convincing, otherwise the story may never be written."

Scott Ashby

"Just what I needed," Ambrose said, "Not only is there a soul on the line, but you want me to clean up a time paradox at the same time."

"Something like that," Mary agreed. "So be here at ten to get your costume, your information packet, and your language and culture injection, so you'll be ready to go at one."

Ambrose growled his assent and hung up the phone.

He chuntered under his breath all the way home, muttering unprintable phrases and casting unkind – though likely true – aspersions about his upcoming client, the redoubtable Mr. Ebenezer Scrooge.

How was he supposed to make a difference in this case? He felt much as he imagined Jonah felt on the way to Nineveh; but then, he mused, Jonah had gotten some pretty good results, once he'd gotten over himself and knuckled down to work on his assignment.

When he'd first come here, ages ago, too long ago to count, really, he'd thought it would be funny – having a ghost playing a ghost, haunting people for their own good, and so he'd picked Ghosts, Inc, as a good place to work.

It had been fun, for the first forever, scaring people straight, but the delight had long since palled.

Maybe it was time for a change. Could you change jobs here? He'd been offered several places of employment and picked one. He didn't know anyone who had changed jobs, how to go about it, or even if it was possible. He'd look into it, soonest. He really was very tired of his job; same thing, over and over, sometimes at night, sometimes in the day, but the routine of it was driving him mad. He'd do this Scrooge job, and then he'd have the week off between Christmas and New Year's and turn in his notice.

It's the Most Wonderful Time for the Fear

It was cold in London, cold enough for even ghosts to take a chill, and Ambrose was glad of the thick traveling cloak the costuming department had provided. The felted wool, still full of the lanolin, managed to cut out most of the wind that would go straight through you, whether or not you were physically there.

He'd appeared to Scrooge, who was, if it were possible, even more disagreeable than the man Dickens had portrayed, and he'd possibly overplayed his role in shoving Ebenezer's nose in the misery he'd caused by his vile and unethical business practices. He pointed out how thin Tiny Tim's arms and legs were, and how he still managed to be full of Christian Love and Joy, despite the fact that the small boy had to beg to help his family, was dying of something-or-other, and his entire life was miserable because of his lameness. And that most of his problems could be solved with just a little more money.

Ambrose had also, of course, showed the slimy git that his nephew still loved him and wanted Ebenezer to be part of his life.

His role fulfilled, he'd returned to Heaven, and the offices of Ghosts, Inc.

He didn't know whether or not he'd made any changes in Ebenezer's attitudes – in the book, that bit didn't happen until the future ghost scared the snot out of him. Ambrose would get a completion report sometime next week…no, the week after next, as all ghosts got Christmas Week off.

He changed his costume for his usual clothing, and hurried home to help his wife with anything that was left to do for Christmas.

Scott Ashby

And he'd be asking about reassignment when he returned to the office in the new year. It wasn't urgent, but when he couldn't even come up with Christmas Spirit for a real Scrooge, it was probably time to move on to another job, at least for a while.

I Saw Three Spirits Come Phasing In

Kaki Olsen

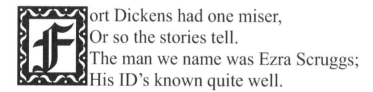ort Dickens had one miser,
Or so the stories tell.
The man we name was Ezra Scruggs;
His ID's known quite well.

His brilliant mind did clever jobs –
Stories were his fame,
For many children, grown-ups, too,
Were intrigued by his games.

He'd carry every player off
Into the worlds of lore,
Each level now more thrilling
Than those that came before.

"The game is free to all," he said,
"But there's a little catch.
IF you wish to truly play,
Upgrade with this new patch."

I Saw Three Spirits Come Phasing In

Resisting a new toy is hard
Even in the best of hours,
But this upgrade needs income
Beyond the parents' powers.

It's not that they did not work hard
To haggle, buy, or barter;
Scruggs wanted more than credit
Which made each upgrade harder.

The powers that be made their appeals,
Which fell on listening ears.
'Twas First Christmas at the Fort
An economy'd take years.

Most merchants made concessions,
Refused IOUs outright
So children of this brave new world
Could enjoy the holy night.

Old Scruggs – he sneered at all of that
And planned temptations plenty:
A tempting new VR campaign
And Scruggsplay, version 20.

He'd give his people Christmas Day,
But summon them at dawn
To roll out the new features
For the game play must go on.

Kaki Olsen

With satisfaction in his mind,
He went to sleep that night –
But a game alert awoke him
To a horrifying sight.

The interface had somehow glitched
And to his groggy view,
He noticed an old NPC,
Phased out in version 2.

This waif had been an afterthought –
A chatty girl who said
She was the baker Marley;
But he knew Marley was dead.

She shouldn't have arrived this night
Or any for that matter,
But she appeared to stare at him
And at once began to chatter.

"Why, Mr. Scruggs, you've lost your way,
Forgot to love the game.
It'll lead you to disaster,
Or Marley's not my name.

"I'm sure that we can fix this
With a careful set of tweaks,
We'll have to stay up all the night
Or this problem could last weeks."

He tried to leave – exit the mode –

I Saw Three Spirits Come Phasing In

Rebooted in the night;
And her satisfaction showed
When Marley stayed in sight.

"Fine, fine," he grumbled to the screen,
"It's not as if you're here.
I'm obviously dreaming or
I've eaten something queer.

"I'll find the glitch and fix it.
I'll resolve this in a trice.
There'll be no room for errors;
The results will be quite nice."

Marley didn't answer then,
But reached a hand to him.
He typed commands to follow her
On a slightly hopeful whim.

There was no choice to access code,
So he played the usual path.
He could find the error quick
And release his coding wrath.

But, with Marley at his side,
He wandered far and near
In search of something out of place
That didn't belong here.

The early build was lovely
And quite simple in design.

Kaki Olsen

The music was enchanting
And the graphics crude, but fine.

"You loved this place, you know it,"
Marley commented just then.
"You kept this as the first save point
Right up to Version 10."

"It was no use to me," Scruggs scoffed
With an appraising glance around.
"No Easter eggs or hidden jewels,
No profit could be found."

"But it was good and pure," she said,
"The welcome place was great."
"A wasteland bare of profit,
Obsolete by Version 8."

It was then he found a clear mistake,
A flaw he'd quickly fix.
When Marley wasn't looking,
He accessed code with clever tricks.

Little effort was required
To escape the newbie realm –
He found himself in Version 19,
Feeling smug if overwhelmed.

There was nothing simple in this place.
The tale was quite advanced.
A quest or skip code was the cost

I Saw Three Spirits Come Phasing In

To move on with a chance.

Marley did not find him here,
But his loyal squire did.
He heaped abuse upon the lad
Who no longer was a kid.

"There's something out of order here –
It's your doing, I just know it.
We'll have to find escape routes, so
Pay attention or we'll blow it."

The squire gibbered, apologized;
His tries feeble at their best –
Designed to be apprentice
And not lead his own knight's quest.

Scruggs made his way from point to point,
With a deft and practiced hand,
This was his virtual paradise,
The world his to command.

But as he traveled far and near,
He noted one more flaw:
There were many questing players,
But little joy was what he saw.

"This game is on the cutting edge,"
To his squire he griped.
"The upgrades are flawless here."
"Yes, but free play is now tripe."

162

Kaki Olsen

The squire shouldn't speak so bold
To one above his station,
But his duty was to serve his Lord
So he gave this explanation:

"Players are few and far between,
Though willing to shell out.
They pay the price to move along,
But their purpose is in doubt.

"Are they here for love of play?
Most would answer, 'no.'
The simpler game, with purpose,
Is a better way to go."

"A game for fools," Scruggs bleated.
The squire seemed sympathetic.
"This mode's high definition."
"Without fun, it's just pathetic."

Scruggs snuck off without delay
'Cause his over-honest servant
Was proving to be tiresome
Though his input was quite fervent.

Escaping was a simple thing,
He'd done it lots before.
He moved on to the newest build,
But questioned now, "What for?"

I Saw Three Spirits Come Phasing In

If the latest tricks and updates brought
No joy, but just a profit,
He begged himself to halt this world.
He wanted to get off it.

But there were better things ahead.
New portals, new dimensions.
This would surely bring them back.
He'd had the best intentions.

It would take some folks a year
To earn the needed tokens,
They could join top playing guilds –
More joy would be awoken.

There was no squire or Marley yet
To point out the new magic.
The build was just half-finished
And the loneliness was tragic.

Scruggs looked upon V. 20
With an expert gamer's eye –
He saw no whimsy in this game
And knew the reason why.

This midnight glitch had called to mind
The reasons he had started.
He'd once been young and much enthused.
He'd even been light-hearted.

There was value that he'd seen tonight

Kaki Olsen

In things without a cost.
There was joy in things without the frills,
Though that message had been lost.

If he could turn his mind and game
To what he'd built at first,
He'd recall what he'd forgot
And feel his life less cursed.

Without another look around,
He left the game post-haste,
Then entered Version 2 and hoped
Marley'd not gone to waste.

"You're back!" she cried. "I missed you so,
But you have naught to fear.
For there's a quest in this small land
And you can come home here."

"Good Marley," Scruggs said with a smile,
"I never mean to go.
This home is one of greatest worth."
"Yes, I told you so.

"You've learned your lesson as I hoped
And I'm eager to assist
In building more upon this game
And showing what you missed."

"Later," he said. "It's time for sleep
But when the next day starts,

I Saw Three Spirits Come Phasing In

I'll know this Christmas lesson
And keep it daily in my heart."

The game was down for a whole week
And many parents fretted.
But V. 20 was free on morning 8
And the wait was not regretted.

Old Scruggs had taken all they loved
And expanded it with pride –
The new rewards were free for all
And Scruggs was on their side.

As promised, he performed each task
With whimsy as his goal.
He kept the spirit all year round,
Or so the tale is told.

Sleep in Kryosleep Peace

Scott Ashby

ight-year-old Jeremy was ready for adventure. He was going to get it, too. It was two weeks before Christmas, but he wouldn't be spending the holiday on Earth. In fact, he wouldn't have Christmas on Earth ever again. It was exciting in a scary sort of way.

Kyra, his five-year-old sister, wasn't excited. She was just plain scared. But heck, she was a girl. Of course she was going to be scared. Life was going to be different forever. It was going to be great.

Jeremy was looking forward to riding in a spaceship. All his friends were jealous. His bestest friend Davy told him that even Clark, the school bully, was jealous of him. They both laughed about that, but not where Clark could hear them. They weren't stupid enough to take that kind of a chance. Jeremy would look dumb getting on a spaceship with a black eye. He was going to miss Davy, but gosh! He was going on a spaceship! That made up for a lot!

Life on Earth had been tough. Dad had lost his job on the space station because something went wrong, and it came crashing down. Luckily, the crew had been rescued, but because the government didn't want to accept the blame for the failed station, they blamed the crew. Jeremy'd heard his mom and dad talking about it. Because the crew had been blamed, nobody would hire anyone from that mission. After two years, their savings were gone.

Then a new company had contacted Dad. A new planet, Pharmbase 2, had been discovered. The company wanted to mine some mineral on it that was rare but important. They were hiring families for a colonization mission. Jeremy heard his parents talking about it. He sat thinking for a long time. He didn't understand part of what they said, but it sounded like their family was moving to Pharmbase 2.

Mom started packing a crate Dad brought home. There was a weight limit for each family, so Mom was weighing each item as she packed it in the box.

Jeremy could only take one small toy and two books. Kyra could only have her doll with one change of clothes for it. Mom promised they'd get cloth to make Kyra's doll some new clothes once they were on Pharmbase 2.

Jeremy's parents explained about moving and what Kryosleep was, but Jeremy was a little scared. No, a lot scared.

Dad had hugged him and said, "Trust me, Son. I love you and wouldn't put us in any danger. When they wake us up, we'll feel the same as we do right now. You won't even have grown any taller. They'll wake us up just before we're ready to land. You'll be able to see that. Won't that be something to tell your grandchildren!" Then he ruffled Jeremy's hair and they had a ten-second tickle fight like they always did when his Dad messed up his hair.

Then Mom squeezed him. Gee whiz, she squeezed him so

tight maybe she thought he was going to walk all the way there from how tight she squeezed. She kissed him on the cheek and said she loved him more than anything.

The next morning, Jeremy's family took a skimmer to the spaceport and boarded the shuttle that would take them to the spaceship. When they got there, a lady showed them where to check in.

Their family was taken to a small room. Mom only had time to give them each one more spine-cruncher hug before a med tech came to take Jeremy and Kyra to a different room. There were rows of beds inside clear plastic tubes. The med tech pointed at a bed for each and told them to lay down. Kyra gave him a wave, but her eyes were wide open with white showing all around, and Jeremy knew she was as afraid as he was deep down – but he was excited, too. She wasn't.

Jeremy smiled really big and gave her a thumbs-up sign so she wouldn't be so scared. She smiled back, then lay down on the skinny bed. Jeremy did the same. The med tech hooked a bunch of wires to them and to the tubes. Jeremy watched a screen start to stream graphs and data, and then the med tech patted him on the shoulder and closed the tube.

Jeremy could feel a cool breeze skim across his forehead. He knew then he'd have plenty of air to breathe; he relaxed as they started to move his bed to a different place.

Kyra put her hand on the tube, as though she was trying to reach him. He smiled at her and waved. She nodded, and then lay flat as the men wheeled her past his tube.

They moved his bed to a different room. It looked like library with shelves full of books, but instead of books, each slot held one of the tube beds with a person inside.

He wondered how he'd feel when he woke up. Would he

remember his dreams? He had fun dreams where he was the hero and helped save people from threatening monsters or aliens.

Jeremy felt himself getting tired. As his bed slid into the bookshelf, he wondered; in two weeks it would be Christmas. When he woke up, would it still be two weeks before Christmas? He had no gifts to give. Suddenly, he was a little nervous about that, feeling like maybe he'd be letting his family down.

It was hard to hold his eyes open. He took in a deep breath and relaxed. That was all.

Two Years Later

Jeremy lay in bed, but kept his eyes closed. He heard noises, but he'd been having a neat dream. He couldn't let Mom know he was awake. He wanted to keep dreaming.

The noises got louder. The dream unicorn he was riding disappeared. Rats.

He may as well get up. If he didn't, Mom would wiggle his shoulder. Or Dad would grab Jeremy's big toe and shake his foot. He tried to sit up.

"Whoa, young fella, hold still."

That didn't sound like Dad. He opened his eyes.

Jeremy saw a man as old as Grandpa outside a plastic cover over his bed. He blinked. He wasn't in his own bed. Where was he?

The old man held up a finger and winked.

"I'm Georgie. Hold on; when it's safe, I'll open your pod and help you." He looked back at the monitor.

Jeremy saw a speaker just above his head and knew that's why he could hear the man outside of the plastic cover.

Georgie watched and then nodded. "Lay still and I'll open

you up. Just sit up. Don't try to climb out yet. You've been asleep for two years. Your legs may not want to hold your weight."

Jeremy heard locks being flipped open; then, the plastic cover was lifted off. He sat up and looked around. Seeing a bunch of plastic tubes with empty beds, he remembered about getting onto the spaceship and being put to sleep. He didn't feel tired and wanted to hop down, go exploring.

"Is my sister Kyra awake yet?"

"Yes. She's getting up now." He pointed across the room.

Jeremy saw Kyra, being steadied by a lady as she stepped onto the floor. She wobbled; the lady helped her stand.

Kyra looked up and saw him. He grinned and waved; she smiled back. It seemed to help her because she pushed upright and stood up straight.

"Come on now, young fella," Georgie said, reaching out a hand to steady Jeremy. "Let your legs dangle over the edge of the bed. When I give you the signal, I'll help you stand. Wait for my signal, though. The boss wouldn't like you to go too fast and end up falling on your face. Easy does it."

Jeremy complied. He wanted to hop down and run over to Kyra, but his legs felt like plascrete and he didn't want to move.

Georgie massaged his lower legs and then helped Jeremy ease his feet to the floor. His legs weren't plascrete; they were flexibands, wobbly and stupid, like somebody had removed his bones while he'd been asleep.

With Georgie's help, he took a step, then another. It wasn't long before he was standing straight and feeling more like his old self, ready to run down the street.

He and Kyra walked towards each other and met in the

middle. She threw her arms around him and squashed him to her. It was kind of like his mom's last hug. He patted Kyra on the back and then stepped to her side.

"Are our parents awake?" he asked Georgie.

"Yesterday. Sammy will take you to them. They're anxious to see you." He waved a med tech over and gave him instructions for their family pod.

As they walked, Jeremy could feel his body adjusting, getting stronger. Kyra walked like she always did, too.

"What day is it?" he asked Sammy.

"Do you mean day of the week, month, or what year we're in?" Sammy grinned.

Jeremy felt the man wanted to ruffle his hair like his dad did. He ducked away just a little and then answered.

"Month and day."

"It's Christmas Eve. Your parents wanted to get ready for you."

Jeremy looked at him. Sammy laughed. "I'm not saying a word. You'll see soon enough."

As they walked, Jeremy thought about not having presents for his family, and wondered what he could do about that. Maybe Dad would have an idea.

Sammy put his hand on a circle on a blue door where the handle should be. It made a bell sound. Sammy leaned close to a wall box by the edge of the door. "Jeremy and Kyra are here."

The door opened and Jeremy was swept into his dad's arms and swung around as though he was three years old, but right now, it felt perfect. He looked over his dad's shoulder, and saw Mom hugging Kyra tightly, and they were crying. Girls!

Scott Ashby

Dad put him down, rumpled his hair, and they had a ten-second tickle fest before Mom grabbed him and hugged him so hard he thought she'd break his ribs. His neck got wet with her tears and she laughed and wiped off his neck with her shirt sleeve. She pointed behind him and whispered, "Look."

Jeremy looked and there on the wall was a hologram of a Christmas tree with ornaments. Lights were twinkling away, just like their old tree on Earth.

"My darling children," Mom said, and Dad put his arm around her. Jeremy thought he did that so Mom wouldn't start bawling again. Dad always kept Mom's tender heart from making her cry too much. Jeremy appreciated that.

"It's Christmas Eve," Mom said, "but we were so restricted on weight, there wasn't much room for anything extra. We were able to bring just one thing for each of you."

Dad handed Jeremy a skinny package. Mom handed Kyra a small box.

Kyra's box held a sewing kit and some pieces of fabric to make clothes for her doll. Kyra's face shined and her smile was as big as her mouth could stretch.

"Go on, Son, open yours."

Jeremy opened his gift to find a small knife with a sheath that could attach to a belt. The sheath was leather...real leather. It had his name on it. Wow! He bet his own smile was as big as Kyra's. He could hardly wait until he showed it to Davy. Suddenly Jeremy remembered he wasn't on Earth anymore. Davy had been left behind.

Then Jeremy had a really good thought. Clark wasn't here, either. Jeremy would never have to worry about another black eye from the bully. Being in Kryosleep for two years had been worth it. Life was going to be peaceful from here on

Sleep in Kryosleep Peace

out. It was a Merry Christmas after all.

About the Authors

Kaki Olsen

Kaki Olsen has written tales in several genres, but she can't stop herself from coming back to retellings. She currently lives far from what she calls home and can often be found preaching the good word of the Boston Red Sox. When not in her home office, she enjoys making music or traveling the world.

Scott Ashby

Scott Ashby loves to write fantasy and science fiction. He lives and works in Gilbert, Arizona in his bedroom office. Like most computer geeks, he doesn't really notice the passing of hours, or days, so long as food arrives on a regular schedule. When not at the computer, Scott enjoys board games, hiking, and letterboxing.

Connect with us online

Kaki Olsen

Website: kakiolsencreative.com
Twitter: KakiOCreative
Facebook: Kaki Olsen

Scott Ashby

Website: electric-scroll.com
Email: s-ashby@electric-scroll.com
Facebook: Scott Ashby